. . .

E D I T H   W H A R T O N

ETHAN FROME
AND OTHER STORIES

an imprint of
RUNNING PRESS
Philadelphia • London

Ethan Frome is reprinted from the first edition, published in 1911 by Charles
Scribner's Sons, New York. "The Other Two" and "The Dilettante" are reprinted
from the first edition of *The Descent of Man and Other Stories*, published in 1904
by Charles Scribner's Sons, New York. "Xingu" is reprinted from the first edition
of *Xingu and Other Stories*, published in 1916 by Charles Scribner's Sons, New
York. All spellings and punctuation are preserved as they appeared in the
original editions, except for obvious typographical errors.

The essay by Harold Bloom is reprinted from *Modern Critical Views:
Edith Wharton*, © 1986 by Chelsea House Publishers. Reprinted
by permission of Chelsea House Publishers.

Cover illustration: Detail of black-and-white photograph reprinted by
permission of Lilly Library, Indiana University, Bloomington, Indiana.

Library of Congress Cataloging-in-Publication Number 96-67174

ISBN 1-56138-763-0

Cover design by Diane Miljat
Edited by Virginia Mattingly
Typography: ITC Berkeley Oldstyle

Published by Courage Books, an imprint of
Running Press Book Publishers
125 South Twenty-second Street
Philadelphia, Pennsylvania 19103-4399

CONTENTS

. . .

ETHAN FROME

I had the story, bit by bit, from various people, and, as generally happens in such cases, each time it was a different story.

If you know Starkfield, Massachusetts, you know the post-office. If you know the post-office you must have seen Ethan Frome drive up to it, drop the reins on his hollow-backed bay and drag himself across the brick pavement to the white colonnade: and you must have asked who he was.

It was there that, several years ago, I saw him for the first time; and the sight pulled me up sharp. Even then he was the most striking figure in Starkfield, though he was but the ruin of a man. It was not so much his great height that marked him, for the "natives" were easily singled out by their lank longitude from the stockier foreign breed: it was the careless powerful look he had, in spite of a lameness checking each step like the jerk of a chain. There was something bleak and unapproachable in his face, and he was so stiffened and grizzled that I took him for an old man and was surprised to hear that he was not more than fifty-two. I had this from Harmon Gow, who had driven the stage from Betts-bridge to Starkfield in pre-trolley days and knew the chronicle of all the families on his line.

"He's looked that way ever since he had his smash-up; and that's twenty-four years ago come next February," Harmon threw out between reminiscent pauses.

The "smash-up" it was—I gathered from the same informant—which, besides drawing the red gash across Ethan Frome's forehead, had so shortened and warped his right side that it cost him a visible effort to take the few steps from his buggy to the post-office window. He used to drive in from his farm every day at about noon, and as that was my own hour for fetching my mail I often passed him in the porch or stood beside him while we waited on the motions of the distributing hand behind the grating. I noticed that, though he came so punctually, he seldom received anything but a copy of the *Bettsbridge Eagle*, which he put without a glance into his sagging pocket. At intervals, however, the post-master would hand him an envelope addressed to Mrs. Zenobia—or Mrs.

Zeena—Frome, and usually bearing conspicuously in the upper left-hand corner the address of some manufacturer of patent medicine and the name of his specific. These documents my neighbour would also pocket without a glance, as if too much used to them to wonder at their number and variety, and would then turn away with a silent nod to the post-master.

Every one in Starkfield knew him and gave him a greeting tempered to his own grave mien; but his taciturnity was respected and it was only on rare occasions that one of the older men of the place detained him for a word. When this happened he would listen quietly, his blue eyes on the speaker's face, and answer in so low a tone that his words never reached me; then he would climb stiffly into his buggy, gather up the reins in his left hand and drive slowly away in the direction of his farm.

"It was a pretty bad smash-up?" I questioned Harmon, looking after Frome's retreating figure, and thinking how gallantly his lean brown head, with its shock of light hair, must have sat on his strong shoulders before they were bent out of shape.

"Wust kind," my informant assented. "More'n enough to kill most men. But the Fromes are tough. Ethan'll likely touch a hundred."

"Good God!" I exclaimed. At the moment, Ethan Frome, after climbing to his seat, had leaned over to assure himself of the security of a wooden box—also with a druggist's label on it—which he had placed in the back of the buggy, and I saw his face as it probably looked when he thought himself alone. "*That* man touch a hundred? He looks as if he was dead and in hell now!"

Harmon drew a slab of tobacco from his pocket, cut off a wedge and pressed it into the leather pouch of his cheek. "Guess he's been in Starkfield too many winters. Most of the smart ones get away."

"Why didn't *he*?"

"Somebody had to stay and care for the folks. There warn't ever anybody but Ethan. Fust his father—then his mother—then his wife."

"And then the smash up?"

Harmon chuckled sardonically. "That's so. He *had* to stay then."

"I see. And since then they've had to care for him?"

Harmon thoughtfully passed his tobacco to the other cheek. "Oh, as to that: I guess it's always Ethan done the caring."

Though Harmon Gow developed the tale as far as his mental and moral reach permitted there were perceptible gaps between his facts, and I had the sense that the deeper meaning of the story was in the gaps. But one phrase stuck in my memory and served as the nucleus about which I grouped my subsequent inferences: "Guess he's been in Starkfield too many winters."

Before my own time there was up I had learned to know what that meant. Yet I had come in the degenerate day of trolley, bicycle and rural delivery, when communication was easy between the scattered mountain villages, and the bigger towns in the valleys, such as Bettsbridge and Shadd's Falls, had libraries, theatres and Y.M.C.A. halls to which the youth of the hills could descend for recreation. But when winter shut down on Starkfield, and the village lay under a sheet of snow perpetually renewed from the pale skies, I began to see what life there—or rather its negation—must have been in Ethan Frome's young manhood.

I had been sent up by my employers on a job connected with the big power-house at Corbury Junction, and a long-drawn carpenters' strike had so delayed the work that I found myself anchored at Starkfield—the nearest habitable spot—for the best part of the winter. I chafed at first, and then, under the hypnotising effect of routine, gradually began to find a grim satisfaction in the life. During the early part of my stay I had been struck by the contrast between the vitality of the climate and the deadness of the community. Day by day, after the December snows were over, a blazing blue sky poured down torrents of light and air on the white landscape, which gave them back in an intenser glitter. One would have supposed that such an atmosphere must quicken the emotions as well as the blood; but it seemed to produce no change except that of retarding still more the sluggish pulse of Starkfield. When I had been there a little longer, and had seen this phase of crystal clearness followed by long stretches of sunless cold; when the storms of February had pitched their white tents about the devoted village and the wild cavalry of March winds had charged down to their support; I began to understand why Starkfield emerged from its six months' siege like a starved garrison capitulating without quarter. Twenty years earlier the means of resistance must have been far fewer, and the enemy in command of almost all the lines of access between the beleaguered villages; and, considering these things, I felt the sinister force of Harmon's phrase: "Most of the smart ones get away." But if that were the case, how could any combination of obstacles have hindered the flight of a man like Ethan Frome?

During my stay at Starkfield I lodged with a middle-aged widow colloquially known as Mrs. Ned Hale. Mrs. Hale's father had been the village lawyer of the previous generation, and "lawyer Varnum's house," where my landlady still lived with her mother, was the most considerable mansion in the village. It stood at one end of the main street, its classic portico and small-paned windows looking down a flagged path between Norway spruces to the slim white steeple of the Congregational church. It was clear that the Varnum fortunes were at the ebb, but the two women did what they could to preserve a decent dignity; and Mrs. Hale, in particular, had a certain wan refinement not out of keeping with her pale old-fashioned house.

In the "best parlour," with its black horse-hair and mahogany weakly illuminated by a gurgling Carcel lamp, I listened every evening to another and more delicately shaded version of the Starkfield chronicle. It was not that Mrs. Ned Hale felt, or affected, any social superiority to the people about her; it was only that the accident of a finer sensibility and a little more education had put just enough distance between herself and her neighbours to enable her to judge them with detachment. She was not unwilling to exercise this faculty, and I had great hopes of getting from her the missing facts of Ethan Frome's story, or rather such a key to his character as should co-ordinate the facts I knew. Her mind was a store-house of innocuous anecdote and any question about her acquaintances brought forth a volume of detail; but on the subject of Ethan Frome I found her unexpectedly reticent. There was no hint of disapproval in her reserve; I merely felt in her an insurmountable reluctance to speak of him or his affairs, a low "Yes, I knew them both . . . it was awful . . ." seeming to be the utmost concession that her distress could make to my curiosity.

So marked was the change in her manner, such depths of sad initiation did it imply, that, with some doubts as to my delicacy, I put the case anew to my village oracle, Harmon Gow; but got for my pains only an uncomprehending grunt.

"Ruth Varnum was always as nervous as a rat; and, come to think of it, she was the first one to see 'em after they was picked up. It happened right below lawyer Varnum's, down at the bend of the Corbury road, just round about the time that Ruth got engaged to Ned Hale. The young folks was all friends, and I guess she just can't bear to talk about it. She's had troubles enough of her own."

All the dwellers in Starkfield, as in more notable communities, had had troubles enough of their own to make them comparatively indifferent to those of their neighbours; and though all conceded that Ethan Frome's had been beyond the common measure, no one gave me an explanation of the look in his face which, as I persisted in thinking, neither poverty nor physical suffering could have put there. Nevertheless, I might have contented myself with the story pieced together from these hints had it not been for the provocation of Mrs. Hale's silence, and—a little later—for the accident of personal contact with the man.

On my arrival at Starkfield, Denis Eady, the rich Irish grocer, who was the proprietor of Starkfield's nearest approach to a livery stable, had entered into an agreement to send me over daily to Corbury Flats, where I had to pick up my train for the Junction. But about the middle of the winter Eady's horses fell ill of a local epidemic. The illness spread to the other Starkfield stables and for a day or two I was put to it to find a means of transport. Then

Harmon Gow suggested that Ethan Frome's bay was still on his legs and that his owner might be glad to drive me over.

I stared at the suggestion. "Ethan Frome? But I've never even spoken to him. Why on earth should he put himself out for me?"

Harmon's answer surprised me still more. "I don't know as he would; but I know he wouldn't be sorry to earn a dollar."

I had been told that Frome was poor, and that the saw-mill and the arid acres of his farm yielded scarcely enough to keep his household through the winter; but I had not supposed him to be in such want as Harmon's words implied, and I expressed my wonder.

"Well, matters ain't gone any too well with him," Harmon said. "When a man's been setting round like a hulk for twenty years or more, seeing things that want doing, it eats inter him, and he loses his grit. That Frome farm was always 'bout as bare's a milk-pan when the cat's been round; and you know what one of them old water-mills is wuth nowadays. When Ethan could sweat over 'em both from sun-up to dark he kinder choked a living out of 'em; but his folks ate up most everything, even then, and I don't see how he makes out now. Fust his father got a kick, out haying, and went soft in the brain, and gave away money like Bible texts afore he died. Then his mother got queer and dragged along for years as weak as a baby; and his wife Zeena, she's always been the greatest hand at doctoring in the county. Sickness and trouble: that's what Ethan's had his plate full up with, ever since the very first helping."

The next morning, when I looked out, I saw the hollow-backed bay between the Varnum spruces, and Ethan Frome, throwing back his worn bearskin, made room for me in the sleigh at his side. After that, for a week, he drove me over every morning to Corbury Flats, and on my return in the afternoon met me again and carried me back through the icy night to Starkfield. The distance each way was barely three miles, but the old bay's pace was slow, and even with firm snow under the runners we were nearly an hour on the way. Ethan Frome drove in silence, the reins loosely held in his left hand, his brown seamed profile, under the helmet-like peak of the cap, relieved against the banks of snow like the bronze image of a hero. He never turned his face to mine, or answered, except in monosyllables, the questions I put, or such slight pleasantries as I ventured. He seemed a part of the mute melancholy landscape, an incarnation of its frozen woe, with all that was warm and sentient in him fast bound below the surface; but there was nothing unfriendly in his silence. I simply felt that he lived in a depth of moral isolation too remote for casual access, and I had the sense that his loneliness was not merely the result of his personal plight, tragic as I guessed that to be, but had in it, as Harmon Gow had hinted, the profound accumulated cold of many Starkfield winters.

Only once or twice was the distance between us bridged for a moment; and the glimpses thus gained confirmed my desire to know more. Once I happened to speak of an engineering job I had been on the previous year in Florida, and of the contrast between the winter landscape about us and that in which I had found myself the year before; and to my surprise Frome said suddenly: "Yes: I was down there once, and for a good while afterward I could call up the sight of it in winter. But now it's all snowed under."

He said no more, and I had to guess the rest from the inflection of his voice and his sharp relapse into silence.

Another day, on getting into my train at the Flats, I missed a volume of popular science—I think it was on some recent discoveries in bio-chemistry—which I had carried with me to read on the way. I thought no more about it till I got into the sleigh again that evening, and saw the book in Frome's hand.

"I found it after you were gone," he said.

I put the volume into my pocket and we dropped back into our usual silence; but as we began to crawl up the long hill from Corbury Flats to the Starkfield ridge I became aware in the dusk that he had turned his face to mine.

"There are things in that book that I didn't know the first word about," he said.

I wondered less at his words than at the queer note of

resentment in his voice. He was evidently surprised and slightly aggrieved at his own ignorance.

"Does that sort of thing interest you?" I asked.

"It used to."

"There are one or two rather new things in the book: there have been some big strides lately in that particular line of research." I waited a moment for an answer that did not come; then I said: "If you'd like to look the book through I'd be glad to leave it with you."

He hesitated, and I had the impression that he felt himself about to yield to a stealing tide of inertia; then, "Thank you—I'll take it," he answered shortly.

I hoped that this incident might set up some more direct communication between us. Frome was so simple and straightforward that I was sure his curiosity about the book was based on a genuine interest in its subject. Such tastes and acquirements in a man of his condition made the contrast more poignant between his outer situation and his inner needs, and I hoped that the chance of giving expression to the latter might at least unseal his lips. But something in his past history, or in his present way of living, had apparently driven him too deeply into himself for any casual impulse to draw him back to his kind. At our next meeting he made no allusion to the book, and our intercourse seemed fated to remain as negative and one-sided as if there had been no break in his reserve.

Frome had been driving me over to the Flats for about a week when one morning I looked out of my window into a thick snowfall. The height of the white waves massed against the garden-fence and along the wall of the church showed that the storm must have been going on all night, and that the drifts were likely to be heavy in the open. I thought it probable that my train would be delayed; but I had to be at the power-house for an hour or two that afternoon, and I decided, if Frome turned up, to push through to the Flats and wait there till my train came in. I don't know why I put it in the conditional, however, for I never doubted that Frome would appear. He was not the kind of man to be turned from his business by any commotion of the elements; and at the appointed hour his sleigh glided up through the snow like a stage-apparition behind thickening veils of gauze.

I was getting to know him too well to express either wonder or gratitude at his keeping his appointment; but I exclaimed in surprise as I saw him turn his horse in a direction opposite to that of the Corbury road.

"The railroad's blocked by a freight-train that got stuck in a drift below the Flats," he explained, as we jogged off into the stinging whiteness.

"But look here—where are you taking me, then?"

"Straight to the Junction, by the shortest way," he answered, pointing up School House Hill with his whip.

"To the Junction—in this storm? Why, it's a good ten miles!"

"The bay'll do it if you give him time. You said you had some business there this afternoon. I'll see you get there."

He said it so quietly that I could only answer: "You're doing me the biggest kind of favour."

"That's all right," he rejoined.

Abreast of the schoolhouse the road forked, and we dipped down a lane to the left, between hemlock boughs bent inward to their trunks by the weight of the snow. I had often walked that way on Sundays, and knew that the solitary roof showing through bare branches near the bottom of the hill was that of Frome's saw-mill. It looked exanimate enough, with its idle wheel looming above the black stream dashed with yellow-white spume, and its cluster of sheds sagging under their white load. Frome did not even turn his head as we drove by, and still in silence we began to mount the next slope. About a mile farther, on a road I had never travelled, we came to an orchard of starved apple-trees writhing over a hillside among outcroppings of slate that nuzzled up through the snow like animals pushing out their noses to breathe. Beyond the orchard lay a field or two, their boundaries lost under drifts; and above the fields, huddled against the white immensities of land and sky, one of those lonely New England farm-houses that make the landscape lonelier.

"That's my place," said Frome, with a sideway jerk of his lame elbow; and in the distress and oppression of the scene I did not know what to answer. The snow had ceased, and a flash of watery sunlight exposed the house on the slope above us in all its plaintive ugliness. The black wraith of a deciduous creeper flapped from the porch, and the thin wooden walls, under their worn coat of paint, seemed to shiver in the wind that had risen with the ceasing of the snow.

"The house was bigger in my father's time: I had to take down the 'L,' a while back," Frome continued, checking with a twitch of the left rein the bay's evident intention of turning in through the broken-down gate.

I saw then that the unusually forlorn and stunted look of the house was partly due to the loss of what is known in New England as the "L": that long deep-roofed adjunct usually built at right angles to the main house, and connecting it, by way of store-rooms and tool-house, with the wood-shed and cow-barn. Whether because of its symbolic sense, the image it presents of a life linked with the soil, and enclosing in itself the chief sources of warmth and nourishment, or whether merely because of the con-solatory thought that it enables the dwellers in that harsh climate to get to their morning's work without facing the weather, it is certain that the "L" rather than the house itself seems to be the centre, the actual hearth-stone, of the New England farm. Perhaps this connection of ideas, which had often occurred to me in my rambles about Starkfield, caused me to hear a wistful note in Frome's words, and to see in the diminished dwelling the image of his own shrunken body.

"We're kinder side-tracked here now," he added, "but there was considerable passing before the railroad was carried through to the Flats." He roused the lagging bay with another twitch; then, as if the mere sight of the house had let me too deeply into his confidence for any farther pretence of reserve, he went on slowly: "I've always set down the worst of mother's trouble to that. When she got the rheumatism so bad she couldn't move around she used to sit up there and watch the road by the hour; and one year, when they was six months mending the Bettsbridge pike after the floods, and Harmon Gow had to bring his stage round this way, she picked up so that she used to get down to the gate most days to see him. But after the trains begun running nobody ever come by here to speak of, and mother never could get it through her head what had happened, and it preyed on her right along till she died."

As we turned into the Corbury road the snow began to fall again, cutting off our last glimpse of the house; and Frome's silence fell with it, letting down between us the old veil of reticence. This time the wind did not cease with the return of the snow. Instead, it sprang up to a gale which now and then, from a tattered sky, flung pale sweeps of sunlight over a landscape chaotically tossed. But the bay was as good as Frome's word, and we pushed on to the Junction through the wild white scene.

In the afternoon the storm held off, and the clearness in the west seemed to my inexperienced eye the pledge of a fair evening. I finished my business as quickly as possible, and we set out for Starkfield with a good chance of getting there for supper. But at sunset the clouds gathered again, bringing an earlier night, and the snow began to fall straight and steadily from a sky without wind, in a soft universal diffusion more confusing than the gusts and eddies of the morning. It seemed to be a part of the thickening darkness, to be the winter night itself descending on us layer by layer.

The small ray of Frome's lantern was soon lost in this smothering medium, in which even his sense of direction, and the bay's homing instinct, finally ceased to serve us. Two or three times some ghostly landmark sprang up to warn us that we were astray, and then was sucked back into the mist; and when we finally regained our road the old horse began to show signs of exhaustion. I felt myself to blame for having accepted Frome's offer, and after a short discussion I persuaded him to let me get out of the sleigh and walk along through the snow at the bay's side. In this way we struggled on for another mile or two, and at last reached a point where Frome, peering into what seemed to me formless night, said: "That's my gate down yonder."

The last stretch had been the hardest part of the way. The bitter cold and the heavy going had nearly knocked the wind out of me, and I could feel the horse's side ticking like a clock under my hand.

"Look here, Frome," I began, "there's no earthly use in your going any farther—" but he interrupted me: "Nor you neither. There's been about enough of this for anybody."

I understood that he was offering me a night's shelter at the farm, and without answering I turned into the gate at his side, and followed him to the barn, where I helped him to unharness and bed down the tired horse. When this was done he unhooked the lantern from the sleigh, stepped out again into the night, and called to me over his shoulder: "This way."

Far off above us a square of light trembled through the screen of snow. Staggering along in Frome's wake I floundered toward it, and in the darkness almost fell into one of the deep drifts against the front of the house. Frome scrambled up the slippery steps of the porch, digging a way through the snow with his heavily booted foot. Then he lifted his lantern, found the latch, and led the way into the house. I went after him into a low unlit passage, at the back of which a ladder-like staircase rose into obscurity. On our right a line of light marked the door of the room which had sent its ray across the night; and behind the door I heard a woman's voice droning querulously.

Frome stamped on the worn oil-cloth to shake the snow from his boots, and set down his lantern on a kitchen chair which was the only piece of furniture in the hall. Then he opened the door.

"Come in," he said; and as he spoke the droning voice grew still. . .

It was that night that I found the clue to Ethan Frome, and began to put together this vision of his story. . . . .

CHAPTER 1

The village lay under two feet of snow, with drifts at the windy corners. In a sky of iron the points of the Dipper hung like icicles and Orion flashed his cold fires. The moon had set, but the night was so transparent that the white house-fronts between the elms looked gray against the snow, clumps of bushes made black stains on it, and the basement windows of the church sent shafts of yellow light far across the endless undulations.

Young Ethan Frome walked at a quick pace along the deserted street, past the bank and Michael Eady's new brick store and Lawyer Varnum's house with the two black Norway spruces at the gate. Opposite the Varnum gate, where the road fell away toward Corbury valley, the church reared its slim white steeple and narrow peristyle. As the young man walked toward it the upper windows drew a black arcade along the side wall of the building, but from the lower openings, on the side where the ground sloped steeply down to the Corbury road, the light shot its long bars, illuminating many fresh furrows in the track leading to the basement door, and showing, under an adjoining shed, a line of sleighs with heavily blanketed horses.

The night was perfectly still, and the air so dry and pure that it gave little sensation of cold. The effect produced on Frome was rather of a complete absence of atmosphere, as though nothing less tenuous than ether intervened between the white earth under his feet and the metallic dome overhead. "It's like being in an exhausted receiver," he thought. Four or five years earlier he had taken a year's course at a technological college at Worcester, and dabbled in the laboratory with a friendly professor of physics; and the images supplied by that experience still cropped up, at unexpected moments, through the totally different associations of thought in which he had since been living. His father's death, and the misfortunes following it, had put a premature end to Ethan's studies; but though they had not gone far enough to be of much practical use they had fed his fancy and made him aware of huge cloudy meanings behind the daily face of things.

As he strode along through the snow the sense of such meanings glowed in his brain and mingled with the bodily flush produced by his sharp tramp. At the end of the village he paused before the darkened front of the church. He stood there a moment, breathing quickly, and looking up and down the street, in which not another figure moved. The pitch of the Corbury road, below lawyer Varnum's spruces, was the favourite coasting-ground of Starkfield, and on clear evenings the church corner rang till late with the shouts of the coasters; but to-night not a sled darkened the whiteness of the long declivity. The hush of midnight lay on the village, and all its waking life was gathered behind the church windows, from which strains of dance-music flowed with the broad bands of yellow light.

The young man, skirting the side of the building, went down the slope toward the basement door. To keep out of range of the revealing rays from within he made a circuit through the untrodden snow and gradually approached the farther angle of the basement wall. Thence, still hugging the shadow, he edged his way cautiously forward to the nearest window, holding back his straight spare body and craning his neck till he got a glimpse of the room.

Seen thus, from the pure and frosty darkness in which he stood, it seemed to be seething in a mist of heat. The metal reflectors of the gas-jets sent crude waves of light against the whitewashed walls, and the iron flanks of the stove at the end of the hall looked as though they were heaving with volcanic fires. The floor was thronged with girls and young men. Down the side wall facing the window stood a row of kitchen chairs from which the older women had just risen. By this time the music had stopped, and the musicians—a fiddler, and the young lady who played the harmonium on Sundays—were hastily refreshing themselves at one corner of the supper-table which aligned its devastated pie-dishes and ice-cream saucers on the platform at the end of the hall. The guests were preparing to leave, and the tide had already set toward the passage where coats and wraps were hung, when a young man with a sprightly foot and a shock of black hair shot into the middle of the floor and clapped his hands. The signal took instant effect. The musicians hurried to their instruments, the dancers—some already half-muffled for departure—fell into line down each side of the room, the older spectators slipped back to their chairs, and the lively young man, after diving about here and there in the throng, drew forth a girl who had already wound a cherry-coloured "fascinator" about her head, and, leading her up to the end of the floor, whirled her down its length to the bounding tune of a Virginia reel.

Frome's heart was beating fast. He had been straining for a glimpse of the dark head under the cherry-coloured scarf and it vexed him that another eye should have been quicker than his. The leader of the reel, who looked as if he had Irish blood in his veins, danced well, and his partner caught his fire. As she passed down the line, her light figure swinging from hand to hand in circles of increasing swiftness, the scarf flew off her head and stood out behind her shoulders, and Frome, at each turn, caught sight of her laughing panting lips, the cloud of dark hair about her forehead, and the dark eyes which seemed the only fixed points in a maze of flying lines.

The dancers were going faster and faster, and the musicians, to keep up with them, belaboured their instruments like jockeys lashing their mounts on the home-stretch; yet it seemed to the young man at the window that the reel would never end. Now and then he turned his eyes from the girl's face to that of her partner, which, in the exhilaration of the dance, had taken on a look of almost impudent ownership. Denis Eady was the son of Michael Eady, the ambitious Irish grocer, whose suppleness and effrontery had given Starkfield its first notion of "smart" business methods, and whose new brick store testified to the success of the attempt. His son seemed likely to follow in his steps, and was meanwhile applying the same arts to the conquest of the Starkfield maidenhood. Hitherto Ethan Frome had been content to think him a mean fellow; but now he positively invited a horse-whipping. It was strange that the girl did not seem aware of it: that she could lift her rapt face to her dancer's, and drop her hands into his, without appearing to feel the offence of his look and touch.

Frome was in the habit of walking into Starkfield to fetch home his wife's cousin, Mattie Silver, on the rare evenings when some chance of amusement drew her to the village. It was his wife who had suggested, when the girl came to live with them, that such opportunities should be put in her way. Mattie Silver came from Stamford, and when she entered the Fromes' household to act as her cousin Zeena's aid it was thought best, as she came without pay, not to let her feel too sharp a contrast between the life she had left and the isolation of a Starkfield farm. But for this—as Frome sardonically reflected—it would hardly have occurred to Zeena to take any thought for the girl's amusement.

When his wife first proposed that they should give Mattie an occasional evening out he had inwardly demurred at having to do the extra two miles to the village and back after his hard day on the farm; but not long afterward he had reached the point of wishing that Starkfield might give all its nights to revelry.

Mattie Silver had lived under his roof for a year, and from early morning till they met at supper he had frequent chances of seeing her; but no moments in her company were comparable to those when, her arm in his, and her light step flying to keep time with his long stride, they walked back through the night to the farm. He had taken to the girl from the first day, when he had driven over to the Flats to meet her, and she had smiled and waved to him from the train, crying out "You must be Ethan!" as she jumped down with her bundles, while he reflected, looking over her slight person: "She don't look much on house-work, but she ain't a fretter, anyhow." But it was not only that the coming to his house of a bit of hopeful young life was like the lighting of a fire on a cold hearth. The girl was more than the bright serviceable creature he had thought her. She had an eye to see and an ear to hear: he could show her things and tell her things, and taste the bliss of feeling that all he imparted left long reverberations and echoes he could wake at will.

It was during their night walks back to the farm that he felt most intensely the sweetness of this communion. He had always been more sensitive than the people about him to the appeal of natural beauty. His unfinished studies had given form to this sensibility and even in his unhappiest moments field and sky spoke to him with a deep and powerful persuasion. But hitherto the emotion had remained in him as a silent ache, veiling with sadness the beauty that evoked it. He did not even know whether any one else in the world felt as he did, or whether he was the sole victim of this mournful privilege. Then he learned that one other spirit had trembled with the same touch of wonder: that at his side, living under his roof and eating his bread, was a creature to whom he could say: "That's Orion down yonder; the big fellow to the right is Aldebaran, and the bunch of little ones—like bees swarming—they're the Pleiades . . ." or whom he could hold entranced before a ledge of granite thrusting up through the fern while he unrolled the huge panorama of the ice age, and the long dim stretches of succeeding time. The fact that admiration for his learning mingled with Mattie's wonder at what he taught was not the least part of his pleasure. And there were other sensations, less definable but more exquisite, which drew them together with a shock of silent joy: the cold red of sunset behind winter hills, the flight of cloud-flocks over slopes of golden stubble, or the intensely blue shadows of hemlocks on sunlit snow. When she said to him once: "It looks just as if it was painted!" it seemed to Ethan that the art of definition could go no farther, and that words had at last been found to utter his secret soul. . . .

As he stood in the darkness outside the church these memories came back with the poignancy of vanished things. Watching Mattie whirl down the floor from hand to hand he wondered how he could ever have thought that his dull talk interested her. To him, who was never gay but in her presence, her gaiety seemed plain proof of indifference. The face she lifted to her dancers was the same which, when she saw him, always looked like a window that has caught the sunset. He even noticed two or three gestures which, in his fatuity, he had thought she kept for him: a way of throwing her head back when she was amused, as if to taste her laugh before she let it out, and a trick of sinking her lids slowly when anything charmed or moved her.

The sight made him unhappy, and his unhappiness roused his latent fears. His wife had never shown any jealousy of Mattie, but of late she had grumbled increasingly over the house-work and found oblique ways of attracting attention to the girl's inefficiency. Zeena had always been what Starkfield called "sickly," and Frome had to admit that, if she were as ailing as she believed, she needed the help of a stronger arm than the one which lay so lightly in his during the night walks to the farm. Mattie had no natural turn for house-keeping, and her training had done nothing to remedy the defect. She was quick to learn, but forgetful and dreamy, and not disposed to take the matter seriously. Ethan had an idea that if she were to marry a man she was fond of the dormant instinct would wake, and her pies and biscuits become the pride of the county; but domesticity in the abstract did not interest her. At first she was so awkward that he could not help laughing at her; but she laughed with him and that made them better friends. He did his best to supplement her unskilled efforts, getting up earlier than usual to light the kitchen fire, carrying in the wood overnight, and neglecting the mill for the farm that he might help her about the house during the day. He even crept down on Saturday nights to scrub the kitchen floor after the women had gone to bed; and Zeena, one day, had surprised him at the churn and had turned away silently, with one of her queer looks.

Of late there had been other signs of her disfavour, as intangible but more disquieting. One cold winter morning, as he dressed in the dark, his candle flickering in the draught of the ill-fitting window, he had heard her speak from the bed behind him.

"The doctor don't want I should be left without anybody to do for me," she said in her flat whine.

He had supposed her to be asleep, and the sound of her voice had startled him, though she was given to abrupt explosions of speech after long intervals of secretive silence.

He turned and looked at her where she lay indistinctly out-lined under the dark calico quilt, her high-boned face taking a grayish tinge from the whiteness of the pillow.

"Nobody to do for you?" he repeated.

"If you say you can't afford a hired girl when Mattie goes."

Frome turned away again, and taking up his razor stooped to catch the reflection of his stretched cheek in the blotched looking-glass above the wash-stand.

"Why on earth should Mattie go?"

"Well, when she gets married, I mean," his wife's drawl came from behind him.

"Oh, she'd never leave us as long as you needed her," he re-turned, scraping hard at his chin.

"I wouldn't ever have it said that I stood in the way of a poor girl like Mattie marrying a smart fellow like Denis Eady," Zeena answered in a tone of plaintive self-effacement.

Ethan, glaring at his face in the glass, threw his head back to draw the razor from ear to chin. His hand was steady, but the atti-tude was an excuse for not making an immediate reply.

"And the doctor don't want I should be left without anybody," Zeena continued. "He wanted I should speak to you about a girl he's heard about, that might come—"

Ethan laid down the razor and straightened himself with a laugh.

"Denis Eady! If that's all I guess there's no such hurry to look round for a girl."

"Well, I'd like to talk to you about it," said Zeena obstinately.

He was getting into his clothes in fumbling haste. "All right. But I haven't got the time now: I'm late as it is," he returned, hold-ing his old silver turnip-watch to the candle.

Zeena, apparently accepting this as final, lay watching him in silence while he pulled his suspenders over his shoulders and jerked his arms into his coat; but as he went toward the door she said, suddenly and incisively: "I guess you're always late, now you shave every morning."

That thrust had frightened him more than any vague insinuations about Denis Eady. It was a fact that since Mattie Silver's coming he had taken to shaving every day; but his wife always seemed to be asleep when he left her side in the winter darkness, and he had stupidly assumed that she would not notice any change in his appearance. Once or twice in the past he had been faintly disquieted by Zenobia's way of letting things happen without seeming to remark them, and then, weeks afterward, in a casual phrase, revealing that she had all along taken her notes and drawn her inferences. Of late, however, there had been no room in his thoughts for such vague apprehensions. Zeena herself, from an oppressive reality, had faded into an insubstantial shade. All his life was lived in the sight and sound of Mattie Silver, and he could no longer conceive of its being otherwise. But now, as he stood outside the church, and saw Mattie spinning down the floor with Denis Eady, a throng of disregarded hints and menaces wove their cloud about his brain. . .

CHAPTER 2

As the dancers poured out of the hall Frome, drawing back behind the projecting storm-door, watched the segregation of the grotesquely muffled groups, in which a moving lantern ray now and then lit up a face flushed with food and dancing. The villagers, being afoot, were the first to climb the slope to the main street, while the country neighbours packed themselves more slowly into the sleighs under the shed.

"Ain't you riding, Mattie?" a woman's voice called back from the throng about the shed, and Ethan's heart gave a jump. From where he stood he could not see the persons coming out of the hall till they had advanced a few steps beyond the wooden sides of the storm-door; but through its cracks he heard a clear voice answer: "Mercy no! Not on such a night."

She was there, then, close to him, only a thin board between. In another moment she would step forth into the night, and his eyes, accustomed to the obscurity, would discern her as clearly as though she stood in daylight. A wave of shyness pulled him back into the dark angle of the wall, and he stood there in silence instead of making his presence known to her. It had been one of the wonders of their intercourse that from the first, she, the quicker, finer, more expressive, instead of crushing him by the contrast, had given him something of her own ease and freedom; but now he felt as heavy and loutish as in his student days, when he had tried to "jolly" the Worcester girls at a picnic.

He hung back, and she came out alone and paused within a few yards of him. She was almost the last to leave the hall, and she stood looking uncertainly about her as if wondering why he did not show himself. Then a man's figure approached, coming so close to her that under their formless wrappings they seemed merged in one dim outline.

"Gentleman friend gone back on you? Say, Matt, that's tough! No, I wouldn't be mean enough to tell the other girls. I ain't as low-down as that." (How Frome hated his cheap banter!) "But look at here, ain't it lucky I got the old man's cutter down there waiting for us?"

Frome heard the girl's voice, gaily incredulous: "What on earth's your father's cutter doin' down there?"

"Why, waiting for me to take a ride. I got the roan colt too. I kinder knew I'd want to take a ride to-night," Eady, in his triumph, tried to put a sentimental note into his bragging voice.

The girl seemed to waver, and Frome saw her twirl the end of her scarf irresolutely about her fingers. Not for the world would he have made a sign to her, though it seemed to him that his life hung on her next gesture.

"Hold on a minute while I unhitch the colt," Denis called to her, springing toward the shed.

She stood perfectly still, looking after him, in an attitude of tranquil expectancy torturing to the hidden watcher. Frome noticed that she no longer turned her head from side to side, as though peering through the night for another figure. She let Denis Eady lead out the horse, climb into the cutter and fling back the bearskin to make room for her at his side; then, with a swift motion of flight, she turned about and darted up the slope toward the front of the church.

"Good-bye! Hope you'll have a lovely ride!" she called back to him over her shoulder.

Denis laughed, and gave the horse a cut that brought him quickly abreast of her retreating figure.

"Come along! Get in quick! It's as slippery as thunder on this turn," he cried, leaning over to reach out a hand to her.

She laughed back at him: "Good-night! I'm not getting in."

By this time they had passed beyond Frome's earshot and he could only follow the shadowy pantomime of their silhouettes as they continued to move along the crest of the slope above him. He saw Eady, after a moment, jump from the cutter and go toward the girl with the reins over one arm. The other he tried to slip through hers; but she eluded him nimbly, and Frome's heart, which had swung out over a black void, trembled back to safety. A moment later he heard the jingle of departing sleigh bells and discerned a figure advancing alone toward the empty expanse of snow before the church.

In the black shade of the Varnum spruces he caught up with her and she turned with a quick "Oh!"

"Think I'd forgotten you, Matt?" he asked with sheepish glee.

She answered seriously: "I thought maybe you couldn't come back for me."

"Couldn't? What on earth could stop me?"

"I knew Zeena wasn't feeling any too good to-day."

"Oh, she's in bed long ago." He paused, a question struggling in him. "Then you meant to walk home all alone?"

"Oh, I ain't afraid!" she laughed.

They stood together in the gloom of the spruces, an empty world glimmering about them wide and grey under the stars. He brought his question out.

"If you thought I hadn't come, why didn't you ride back with Denis Eady?"

"Why, where *were* you? How did you know? I never saw you!"

Her wonder and his laughter ran together like spring rills in a thaw. Ethan had the sense of having done something arch and ingenious. To prolong the effect he groped for a dazzling phrase, and brought out, in a growl of rapture: "Come along."

He slipped an arm through hers, as Eady had done, and fancied it was faintly pressed against her side; but neither of them moved. It was so dark under the spruces that he could barely see the shape of her head beside his shoulder. He longed to stoop his cheek and rub it against her scarf. He would have liked to stand there with her all night in the blackness. She moved forward a step or two and then paused again above the dip of the Corbury road. Its icy slope, scored by innumerable runners, looked like a mirror scratched by travellers at an inn.

"There was a whole lot of them coasting before the moon set," she said.

"Would you like to come in and coast with them some night?" he asked.

"Oh, *would* you, Ethan? It would be lovely!"

"We'll come to-morrow if there's a moon."

She lingered, pressing closer to his side. "Ned Hale and Ruth Varnum came just as *near* running into the big elm at the bottom. We were all sure they were killed." Her shiver ran down his arm. "Wouldn't it have been too awful? They're so happy!"

"Oh, Ned ain't much at steering. I guess I can take you down all right!" he said disdainfully.

He was aware that he was "talking big," like Denis Eady; but his reaction of joy had unsteadied him, and the inflection with which she had said of the engaged couple "They're so happy!" made the words sound as if she had been thinking of herself and him.

"The elm *is* dangerous, though. It ought to be cut down," she insisted.

"Would you be afraid of it, with me?"

"I told you I ain't the kind to be afraid," she tossed back, almost indifferently; and suddenly she began to walk on with a rapid step.

These alterations of mood were the despair and joy of Ethan Frome. The motions of her mind were as incalculable as the flit of a bird in the branches. The fact that he had no right to show his feelings, and thus provoke the expression of hers, made him attach a fantastic importance to every change in her look and tone. Now he thought she understood him, and feared; now he was sure she did not, and despaired. To-night the pressure of accumulated misgivings sent the scale drooping toward despair, and her indifference was the more chilling after the flush of joy into which she had plunged him by dismissing Denis Eady. He mounted School House Hill at her side and walked on in silence till they reached the lane leading to the saw-mill; then the need of some definite assurance grew too strong for him.

"You'd have found me right off if you hadn't gone back to have that last reel with Denis," he brought out awkwardly. He could not pronounce the name without a stiffening of the muscles of his throat.

"Why, Ethan, how could I tell you were there?"

"I suppose what folks say is true," he jerked out at her, instead of answering.

She stopped short, and he felt, in the darkness, that her face was lifted quickly to his. "Why, what do folks say?"

"It's natural enough you should be leaving us," he floundered on, following his thought.

"Is that what they say?" she mocked back at him; then, with a sudden drop of her sweet treble: "You mean that Zeena—ain't suited with me any more?" she faltered.

Their arms had slipped apart and they stood motionless, each seeking to distinguish the other's face.

"I know I ain't anything like as smart as I ought to be," she went on, while he vainly struggled for expression. "There's lots of things a hired girl could do that come awkward to me still—and I haven't got much strength in my arms. But if she'd only tell me I'd try. You know she hardly ever says anything, and sometimes I can see she ain't suited, and yet I don't know why." She turned on him with a sudden flash of indignation. "You'd ought to tell me, Ethan Frome—you'd ought to! Unless *you* want me to go too——"

Unless he wanted her to go too! The cry was balm to his raw wound. The iron heavens seemed to melt and rain down sweetness. Again he struggled for the all-expressive word, and again, his arm in hers, found only a deep "Come along."

They walked on in silence through the blackness of the hemlock-shaded lane, where Ethan's saw-mill gloomed through the night, and out again into the comparative clearness of the fields. On the farther side of the hemlock belt the open country rolled away before them grey and lonely under the stars. Sometimes their way led them under the shade of an overhanging bank or through the thin obscurity of a clump of leafless trees. Here and there a farmhouse stood far back among the fields, mute and cold as a grave-stone. The night was so still that they heard the frozen snow crackle under their feet. The crash of a loaded branch falling far off in the woods reverberated like a musket-shot, and once a fox barked, and Mattie shrank closer to Ethan, and quickened her steps.

At length they sighted the group of larches at Ethan's gate, and as they drew near it the sense that the walk was over brought back his words.

"Then you don't want to leave us, Matt?"

He had to stoop his head to catch her stifled whisper: "Where'd I go, if I did?"

The answer sent a pang through him but the tone suffused him with joy. He forgot what else he had meant to say and pressed her against him so closely that he seemed to feel her warmth in his veins.

"You ain't crying are you, Matt?"

"No, of course I'm not," she quavered.

They turned in at the gate and passed under the shaded knoll where, enclosed in a low fence, the Frome grave-stones slanted at crazy angles through the snow. Ethan looked at them curiously. For years that quiet company had mocked his restlessness, his desire for change and freedom. "We never got away—how should you?" seemed to be written on every headstone; and whenever he went in or out of his gate he thought with a shiver: "I shall just go on living here till I join them." But now all desire for change had vanished, and the sight of the little enclosure gave him a warm sense of continuance and stability.

"I guess we'll never let you go, Matt," he whispered, as though even the dead, lovers once, must conspire with him to keep her; and brushing by the graves, he thought: "We'll always go on living here together, and some day she'll lie there beside me."

He let the vision possess him as they climbed the hill to the house. He was never so happy with her as when he abandoned himself to these dreams. Half-way up the slope Mattie stumbled against some unseen obstruction and clutched his sleeve to steady herself. The wave of warmth that went through him was like the prolongation of his vision. For the first time he stole his arm about her, and she did not resist. They walked on as if they were floating on a summer stream.

Zeena always went to bed as soon as she had had her supper, and the shutterless windows of the house were dark. A dead cucumber-vine dangled from the porch like the crape streamer tied to the door for a death, and the thought flashed through Ethan's brain: "If it was there for Zeena—" Then he had a distinct sight of his wife lying in their bedroom asleep, her mouth slightly open, her false teeth in a tumbler by the bed . . .

They walked around to the back of the house, between the rigid gooseberry bushes. It was Zeena's habit, when they came back late from the village, to leave the key of the kitchen door under the mat. Ethan stood before the door, his head heavy with dreams, his arm still about Mattie. "Matt—" he began, not know-ing what he meant to say.

She slipped out of his hold without speaking, and he stooped down and felt for the key.

"It's not there!" he said, straightening himself with a start.

They strained their eyes at each other through the icy dark-ness. Such a thing had never happened before.

"Maybe she's forgotten it," Mattie said in a tremulous whisper; but both of them knew that it was not like Zeena to forget.

"It might have fallen off into the snow," Mattie continued, after a pause during which they had stood intently listening.

"It must have been pushed off, then," he rejoined in the same tone. Another wild thought tore through him. What if tramps had been there—what if . . .

Again he listened, fancying he heard a distant sound in the house; then he felt in his pocket for a match, and kneeling down, passed its light slowly over the rough edges of snow about the doorstep.

He was still kneeling when his eyes, on a level with the lower panel of the door, caught a faint ray beneath it. Who could be stir-ring in that silent house? He heard a step on the stairs, and again for an instant the thought of tramps tore through him. Then the door opened and he saw his wife.

Against the dark background of the kitchen she stood up tall and angular, one hand drawing a quilted counterpane to her flat breast, while the other held a lamp. The light, on a level with her chin, drew out of the darkness her puckered throat and the pro-jecting wrist of the hand that clutched the quilt, and deepened fantastically the hollows and prominences of her high-boned face under its ring of crimping-pins. To Ethan, still in the rosy haze of his hour with Mattie, the sight came with the intense precision of the last dream before waking. He felt as if he had never before known what his wife looked like.

She drew aside without speaking, and Mattie and Ethan

passed into the kitchen, which had the deadly chill of a vault after the dry cold of the night.

"Guess you forgot about us, Zeena," Ethan joked, stamping the snow from his boots.

"No. I just felt so mean I couldn't sleep."

Mattie came forward, unwinding her wraps, the colour of the cherry scarf in her fresh lips and cheeks. "I'm so sorry, Zeena! Isn't there anything I can do?"

"No; there's nothing." Zeena turned away from her. "You might 'a' shook off that snow outside," she said to her husband.

She walked out of the kitchen ahead of them and pausing in the hall raised the lamp at arm's-length, as if to light them up the stairs.

Ethan paused also, affecting to fumble for the peg on which he hung his coat and cap. The doors of the two bedrooms faced each other across the narrow upper landing, and to-night it was peculiarly repugnant to him that Mattie should see him follow Zeena.

"I guess I won't come up yet awhile," he said, turning as if to go back to the kitchen.

Zeena stopped short and looked at him. "For the land's sake— what are you going to do down here?"

"I've got the mill accounts to go over."

She continued to stare at him, the flame of the unshaded lamp bringing out with microscopic cruelty the fretful lines of her face.

"At this time o' night? You'll ketch your death. The fire's out long ago."

Without answering he moved away toward the kitchen. As he did so his glance crossed Mattie's and he fancied that a fugitive warning gleamed through her lashes. The next moment they sank to her flushed cheeks and she began to mount the stairs ahead of Zeena.

"That's so. It *is* powerful cold down here," Ethan assented; and with lowered head he went up in his wife's wake, and followed her across the threshold of their room.

CHAPTER 3

There was some hauling to be done at the lower end of the wood-lot, and Ethan was out early the next day.

The winter morning was as clear as crystal. The sunrise burned red in a pure sky, the shadows on the rim of the wood-lot were darkly blue, and beyond the white and scintillating fields patches of far-off forest hung like smoke.

It was in the early morning stillness, when his muscles were swinging to their familiar task and his lungs expanding with long draughts of mountain air, that Ethan did his clearest thinking. He and Zeena had not exchanged a word after the door of their room had closed on them. She had measured out some drops from a medicine-bottle on a chair by the bed and, after swallowing them, and wrapping her head in a piece of yellow flannel, had lain down with her face turned away. Ethan undressed hurriedly and blew out the light so that he should not see her when he took his place at her side. As he lay there he could hear Mattie moving about in her room, and her candle, sending its small ray across the landing, drew a scarcely perceptible line of light under his door. He kept his eyes fixed on the light till it vanished. Then the room grew perfectly black, and not a sound was audible but Zeena's asthmatic breathing. Ethan felt confusedly that there were many things he ought to think about, but through his tingling veins and tired brain only one sensation throbbed: the warmth of Mattie's shoulder against his. Why had he not kissed her when he held her there? A few hours earlier he would not have asked himself the question. Even a few minutes earlier, when they had stood alone outside the house, he would not have dared to think of kissing her. But since he had seen her lips in the lamplight he felt that they were his.

Now, in the bright morning air, her face was still before him. It was part of the sun's red and of the pure glitter on the snow. How the girl had changed since she had come to Starkfield! He remembered what a colourless slip of a thing she had looked the day he had met her at the station. And all the first winter, how she had shivered with cold when the northerly gales shook the thin clapboards and the snow beat like hail against the loose-hung windows!

He had been afraid that she would hate the hard life, the cold and loneliness; but not a sign of discontent escaped her. Zeena took the view that Mattie was bound to make the best of Stark-field since she hadn't any other place to go to; but this did not strike Ethan as conclusive. Zeena, at any rate, did not apply the principle in her own case.

He felt all the more sorry for the girl because misfortune had, in a sense, indentured her to them. Mattie Silver was the daughter of a cousin of Zenobia Frome's, who had inflamed his clan with mingled sentiments of envy and admiration by descending from the hills to Connecticut, where he had married a Stamford girl and succeeded to her father's thriving "drug" business. Unhappily Orin Silver, a man of far-reaching aims, had died too soon to prove that the end justifies the means. His accounts revealed merely what the means had been; and these were such that it was fortunate for his wife and daughter that his books were examined only after his impressive funeral. His wife died of the disclosure, and Mattie, at twenty, was left alone to make her way on the fifty dollars obtained from the sale of her piano. For this purpose her equipment, though varied, was inadequate. She could trim a hat, make molasses candy, recite "Curfew shall not ring to-night," and play "The Lost Chord" and a pot-pourri from "Carmen." When she tried to extend the field of her activities in the direction of stenography and book-keeping her health broke down, and six months on her feet behind the counter of a department store did not tend to restore it. Her nearest relations had been induced to place their savings in her father's hands, and though, after his death, they ungrudgingly acquitted themselves of the Christian duty of returning good for evil by giving his daughter all the advice at their disposal, they could hardly be expected to supple-ment it by material aid. But when Zenobia's doctor recommended her looking about for some one to help her with the house-work the clan instantly saw the chance of exacting a compensation from Mattie. Zenobia, though doubtful of the girl's efficiency, was tempted by the freedom to find fault without much risk of losing her; and so Mattie came to Starkfield.

Zenobia's fault-finding was of the silent kind, but not the less penetrating for that. During the first months Ethan alternately burned with the desire to see Mattie defy her and trembled with fear of the result. Then the situation grew less strained. The pure air, and the long summer hours in the open, gave back life and elasticity to Mattie, and Zeena, with more leisure to devote to her complex ailments, grew less watchful of the girl's omissions; so that Ethan, struggling on under the burden of his barren farm and failing saw-mill, could at least imagine that peace reigned in his house.

There was really, even now, no tangible evidence to the contrary; but since the previous night a vague dread had hung on his sky-line. It was formed of Zeena's obstinate silence, of Mattie's sudden look of warning, of the memory of just such fleeting imperceptible signs as those which told him, on certain stainless mornings, that before night there would be rain.

His dread was so strong that, man-like, he sought to postpone certainty. The hauling was not over till mid-day, and as the lumber was to be delivered to Andrew Hale, the Starkfield builder, it was really easier for Ethan to send Jotham Powell, the hired man, back to the farm on foot, and drive the load down to the village himself. He had scrambled up on the logs, and was sitting astride of them, close over his shaggy grays, when, coming between him and their steaming necks, he had a vision of the warning look that Mattie had given him the night before.

"If there's going to be any trouble I want to be there," was his vague reflection, as he threw to Jotham the unexpected order to unhitch the team and lead them back to the barn.

It was a slow trudge home through the heavy fields, and when the two men entered the kitchen Mattie was lifting the coffee from the stove and Zeena was already at the table. Her husband stopped short at sight of her. Instead of her usual calico wrapper and knitted shawl she wore her best dress of brown merino, and above her thin strands of hair, which still preserved the tight undulations of the crimping-pins, rose a hard perpendicular bonnet, as to which Ethan's clearest notion was that he had to pay five dollars for it at the Bettsbridge Emporium. On the floor beside her stood his old valise and a bandbox wrapped in newspapers.

"Why, where are you going, Zeena?" he exclaimed.

"I've got my shooting pains so bad that I'm going over to Bettsbridge to spend the night with Aunt Martha Pierce and see that new doctor," she answered in a matter-of-fact tone, as if she had said she was going into the store-room to take a look at the preserves, or up to the attic to go over the blankets.

In spite of her sedentary habits such abrupt decisions were not without precedent in Zeena's history. Twice or thrice before she had suddenly packed Ethan's valise and started off to Bettsbridge, or even Springfield, to seek the advice of some new doctor, and her husband had grown to dread these expeditions because of their cost. Zeena always came back laden with expensive remedies, and her last visit to Springfield had been commemorated by her paying twenty dollars for an electric battery of which she had never been able to learn the use. But for the moment his sense of relief was so great as to preclude all other feelings. He had now no doubt that Zeena had spoken the truth in saying, the night before, that she had sat up because she felt "too mean" to sleep: her abrupt resolve to seek medical advice showed that, as usual, she was wholly absorbed in her health.

As if expecting a protest, she continued plaintively; "If you're too busy with the hauling I presume you can let Jotham Powell drive me over with the sorrel in time to ketch the train at the Flats."

Her husband hardly heard what she was saying. During the winter months there was no stage between Starkfield and Bettsbridge, and the trains which stopped at Corbury Flats were slow and infrequent. A rapid calculation showed Ethan that Zeena could not be back at the farm before the following evening. . . .

"If I'd supposed you'd 'a' made any objection to Jotham Powell's driving me over—" she began again, as though his silence
had implied refusal. On the brink of departure she was always
seized with a flux of words. "All I know is," she continued, "I
can't go on the way I am much longer. The pains are clear away
down to my ankles now, or I'd 'a' walked in to Starkfield on my
own feet, sooner'n put you out, and asked Michael Eady to let me
ride over on his wagon to the Flats, when he sends to meet the
train that brings his groceries. I'd 'a' had two hours to wait in the
station, but I'd sooner 'a' done it, even with this cold, than to have
you say——"

"Of course Jotham'll drive you over," Ethan roused himself to
answer. He became suddenly conscious that he was looking at
Mattie while Zeena talked to him, and with an effort he turned his
eyes to his wife. She sat opposite the window, and the pale light
reflected from the banks of snow made her face look more than
usually drawn and bloodless, sharpened the three parallel creases
between ear and cheek, and drew querulous lines from her thin
nose to the corners of her mouth. Though she was but seven
years her husband's senior, and he was only twenty-eight, she was
already an old woman.

Ethan tried to say something befitting the occasion, but there
was only one thought in his mind: the fact that, for the first time
since Mattie had come to live with them, Zeena was to be away
for a night. He wondered if the girl were thinking of it too. . . .

He knew that Zeena must be wondering why he did not offer
to drive her to the Flats and let Jotham Powell take the lumber to
Starkfield, and at first he could not think of a pretext for not
doing so; then he said: "I'd take you over myself, only I've got to
collect the cash for the lumber."

As soon as the words were spoken he regretted them, not only
because they were untrue—there being no prospect of his receiv-
ing cash payment from Hale—but also because he knew from
experience the imprudence of letting Zeena think he was in funds
on the eve of one of her therapeutic excursions. At the moment,

however, his one desire was to avoid the long drive with her behind the ancient sorrel who never went out of a walk.

Zeena made no reply: she did not seem to hear what he had said. She had already pushed her plate aside, and was measuring out a draught from a large bottle at her elbow.

"It ain't done me a speck of good, but I guess I might as well use it up," she remarked; adding, as she pushed the empty bottle toward Mattie: "If you can get the taste out it'll do for pickles."

CHAPTER 4

As soon as his wife had driven off Ethan took his coat and cap from the peg. Mattie was washing up the dishes, humming one of the dance tunes of the night before. He said "So long, Matt," and she answered gaily "So long, Ethan"; and that was all.

It was warm and bright in the kitchen. The sun slanted through the south window on the girl's moving figure, on the cat dozing in a chair, and on the geraniums brought in from the doorway, where Ethan had planted them in the summer to "make a garden" for Mattie. He would have liked to linger on, watching her tidy up and then settle down to her sewing; but he wanted still more to get the hauling done and be back at the farm before night.

All the way down to the village he continued to think of his return to Mattie. The kitchen was a poor place, not "spruce" and shining as his mother had kept it in his boyhood; but it was surprising what a homelike look the mere fact of Zeena's absence gave it. And he pictured what it would be like that evening, when he and Mattie were there after supper. For the first time they would be alone together indoors, and they would sit there, one on each side of the stove, like a married couple, he in his stocking feet and smoking his pipe, she laughing and talking in that funny way she had, which was always as new to him as if he had never heard her before.

The sweetness of the picture, and the relief of knowing that his fears of "trouble" with Zeena were unfounded, sent up his spirits with a rush, and he, who was usually so silent, whistled and sang aloud as he drove through the snowy fields. There was in him a slumbering spark of sociability which the long Starkfield winters had not yet extinguished. By nature grave and inarticulate, he admired recklessness and gaiety in others and was warmed to the marrow by friendly human intercourse. At Worcester, though he had the name of keeping to himself and not being much of a hand at a good time, he had secretly gloried in being clapped on the back and hailed as "Old Ethe" or "Old Stiff"; and the cessation of such familiarities had increased the chill of his return to Starkfield.

There the silence had deepened about him year by year. Left alone, after his father's accident, to carry the burden of farm and mill, he had had no time for convivial loiterings in the village; and when his mother fell ill the loneliness of the house grew more oppressive than that of the fields. His mother had been a talker in her day, but after her "trouble" the sound of her voice was seldom heard, though she had not lost the power of speech. Sometimes, in the long winter evenings, when in desperation her son asked her why she didn't "say something," she would lift a finger and answer: "Because I'm listening"; and on stormy nights, when the loud wind was about the house, she would complain, if he spoke to her: "They're talking so out there that I can't hear you."

It was only when she drew toward her last illness, and his cousin Zenobia Pierce came over from the next valley to help him nurse her, that human speech was heard again in the house. After the mortal silence of his long imprisonment Zeena's volubility was music in his ears. He felt that he might have "gone like his mother" if the sound of a new voice had not come to steady him. Zeena seemed to understand his case at a glance. She laughed at him for not knowing the simplest sick-bed duties and told him to "go right along out" and leave her to see to things. The mere fact of obeying her orders, of feeling free to go about his business again and talk with other men, restored his shaken balance and magnified his sense of what he owed her. Her efficiency shamed and dazzled him. She seemed to possess by instinct all the household wisdom that his long apprenticeship had not instilled in him. When the end came it was she who had to tell him to hitch up and go for the undertaker, and she thought it "funny" that he had not settled beforehand who was to have his mother's clothes and the sewing-machine. After the funeral, when he saw her preparing to go away, he was seized with an unreasoning dread of being left alone on the farm; and before he knew what he was doing he had asked her to stay there with him. He had often thought since that it would not have happened if his mother had died in spring instead of winter . . .

When they married it was agreed that, as soon as he could straighten out the difficulties resulting from Mrs. Frome's long illness, they would sell the farm and saw-mill and try their luck in a large town. Ethan's love of nature did not take the form of a taste for agriculture. He had always wanted to be an engineer, and to live in towns, where there were lectures and big libraries and "fellows doing things." A slight engineering job in Florida, put in his way during his period of study at Worcester, increased his faith in his ability as well as his eagerness to see the world; and he felt sure that, with a "smart" wife like Zeena, it would not be long before he had made himself a place in it.

Zeena's native village was slightly larger and nearer to the railway than Starkfield, and she had let her husband see from the first that life on an isolated farm was not what she had expected when she married. But purchasers were slow in coming, and while he waited for them Ethan learned the impossibility of transplanting her. She chose to look down on Starkfield, but she could not have lived in a place which looked down on her. Even Bettsbridge or Shadd's Falls would not have been sufficiently aware of her, and in the greater cities which attracted Ethan she would have suffered a complete loss of identity. And within a year of their marriage she developed the "sickliness" which had since made her notable even in a community rich in pathological instances. When she came to take care of his mother she had seemed to Ethan like the very genius of health, but he soon saw that her skill as a nurse had been acquired by the absorbed observation of her own symptoms.

Then she too fell silent. Perhaps it was the inevitable effect of life on the farm, or perhaps, as she sometimes said, it was because Ethan "never listened." The charge was not wholly unfounded. When she spoke it was only to complain, and to complain of things not in his power to remedy; and to check a tendency to impatient retort he had first formed the habit of not answering her, and finally of thinking of other things while she talked. Of late, however, since he had had reasons for observing her more closely, her silence had begun to trouble him. He recalled his mother's growing taciturnity, and wondered if Zeena were also turning "queer." Women did, he knew. Zeena, who had at her fingers' ends the pathological chart of the whole region, had cited many cases of the kind while she was nursing his mother; and he himself knew of certain lonely farm-houses in the neighbourhood where stricken creatures pined, and of others where sudden tragedy had come of their presence. At times, looking at Zeena's shut face, he felt the chill of such forebodings. At other times her silence seemed deliberately assumed to conceal far-reaching intentions, mysterious conclusions drawn from suspicions and resentments impossible to guess. That supposition was even more disturbing than the other; and it was the one which had come to him the night before, when he had seen her standing in the kitchen door.

Now her departure for Bettsbridge had once more eased his mind, and all his thoughts were on the prospect of his evening with Mattie. Only one thing weighed on him, and that was his having told Zeena that he was to receive cash for the lumber. He foresaw so clearly the consequences of this imprudence that with considerable reluctance he decided to ask Andrew Hale for a small advance on his load.

When Ethan drove into Hale's yard the builder was just getting out of his sleigh.

"Hello, Ethe!" he said. "This comes handy."

Andrew Hale was a ruddy man with a big gray moustache and a stubbly double-chin unconstrained by a collar; but his scrupulously clean shirt was always fastened by a small diamond stud. This display of opulence was misleading, for though he did a fairly good business it was known that his easy-going habits and the demands of his large family frequently kept him what Starkfield called "behind." He was an old friend of Ethan's family, and his house one of the few to which Zeena occasionally went, drawn there by the fact that Mrs. Hale, in her youth, had done more "doctoring" than any other woman in Starkfield, and was still a recognised authority on symptoms and treatment.

Hale went up to the grays and patted their sweating flanks.

"Well, sir," he said, "you keep them two as if they was pets."

Ethan set about unloading the logs and when he had finished his job he pushed open the glazed door of the shed which the builder used as his office. Hale sat with his feet up on the stove, his back propped against a battered desk strewn with papers: the place, like the man, was warm, genial and untidy.

"Sit right down and thaw out," he greeted Ethan.

The latter did not know how to begin, but at length he managed to bring out his request for an advance of fifty dollars. The blood rushed to his thin skin under the sting of Hale's astonishment. It was the builder's custom to pay at the end of three months, and there was no precedent between the two men for a cash settlement.

Ethan felt that if he had pleaded an urgent need Hale might have made shift to pay him; but pride, and an instinctive prudence, kept him from resorting to this argument. After his father's death it had taken time to get his head above water, and he did not want Andrew Hale, or any one else in Starkfield, to think he was going under again. Besides, he hated lying; if he wanted the money he wanted it, and it was nobody's business to ask why. He therefore made his demand with the awkwardness of a proud man who will not admit to himself that he is stooping; and he was not much surprised at Hale's refusal.

The builder refused genially, as he did everything else: he treated the matter as something in the nature of a practical joke, and wanted to know if Ethan meditated buying a grand piano or adding a "cupolo" to his house; offering, in the latter case, to give his services free of cost.

Ethan's arts were soon exhausted, and after an embarrassed pause he wished Hale good day and opened the door of the office. As he passed out the builder suddenly called after him: "See here—you ain't in a tight place, are you?"

"Not a bit," Ethan's pride retorted before his reason had time to intervene.

"Well, that's good! Because I *am*, a shade. Fact is, I was going to ask you to give me a little extra time on that payment. Business is pretty slack, to begin with, and then I'm fixing up a little house for Ned and Ruth when they're married. I'm glad to do it for 'em, but it costs." His look appealed to Ethan for sympathy. "The young people like things nice. You know how it is yourself: it's not so long ago since you fixed up your own place for Zeena."

Ethan left the grays in Hale's stable and went about some other business in the village. As he walked away the builder's last phrase lingered in his ears, and he reflected grimly that his seven years with Zeena seemed to Starkfield "not so long."

The afternoon was drawing to an end, and here and there a lighted pane spangled the cold gray dusk and made the snow look whiter. The bitter weather had driven every one indoors and Ethan had the long rural street to himself. Suddenly he heard the brisk play of sleigh-bells and a cutter passed him, drawn by a free-going horse. Ethan recognised Michael Eady's roan colt, and young Denis Eady, in a handsome new fur cap, leaned forward and waved a greeting. "Hello, Ethe!" he shouted and spun on.

The cutter was going in the direction of the Frome farm, and Ethan's heart contracted as he listened to the dwindling bells. What more likely than that Denis Eady had heard of Zeena's departure for Bettsbridge, and was profiting by the opportunity to spend an hour with Mattie? Ethan was ashamed of the storm of jealousy in his breast. It seemed unworthy of the girl that his thoughts of her should be so violent.

He walked on to the church corner and entered the shade of the Varnum spruces, where he had stood with her the night before. As he passed into their gloom he saw an indistinct outline just ahead of him. At his approach it melted for an instant into two separate shapes and then conjoined again, and he heard a kiss, and a half-laughing "Oh!" provoked by the discovery of his presence. Again the outline hastily disunited and the Varnum gate slammed on one half while the other hurried on ahead of him. Ethan smiled at the discomfiture he had caused. What did it matter to Ned Hale and Ruth Varnum if they were caught kissing each other? Everybody in Starkfield knew they were engaged. It pleased Ethan to have surprised a pair of lovers on the spot where he and Mattie had stood with such a thirst for each other in their hearts; but he felt a pang at the thought that these two need not hide their happiness.

He fetched the grays from Hale's stable and started on his long climb back to the farm. The cold was less sharp than earlier in the day and a thick fleecy sky threatened snow for the morrow. Here and there a star pricked through, showing behind it a deep well of blue. In an hour or two the moon would push up over the ridge behind the farm, burn a gold-edged rent in the clouds, and then be swallowed by them. A mournful peace hung on the fields, as though they felt the relaxing grasp of the cold and stretched themselves in their long winter sleep.

Ethan's ears were alert for the jingle of sleigh-bells, but not a sound broke the silence of the lonely road. As he drew near the farm he saw, through the thin screen of larches at the gate, a light twinkling in the house above him. "She's up in her room," he said to himself, "fixing herself up for supper"; and he remembered Zeena's sarcastic stare when Mattie, on the evening of her arrival, had come down to supper with smoothed hair and a ribbon at her neck.

He passed by the graves on the knoll and turned his head to

glance at one of the older headstones, which had interested him deeply as a boy because it bore his name.

SACRED TO THE MEMORY OF

ETHAN FROME AND ENDURANCE HIS WIFE,

WHO DWELLED TOGETHER IN PEACE

FOR FIFTY YEARS.

He used to think that fifty years sounded like a long time to live together; but now it seemed to him that they might pass in a flash. Then, with a sudden dart of irony, he wondered if, when their turn came, the same epitaph would be written over him and Zeena.

He opened the barn-door and craned his head into the obscurity, half-fearing to discover Denis Eady's roan colt in the stall beside the sorrel. But the old horse was there alone, mumbling his crib with toothless jaws, and Ethan whistled cheerfully while he bedded down the grays and shook an extra measure of oats into their mangers. His was not a tuneful throat, but harsh melodies burst from it as he locked the barn and sprang up the hill to the house. He reached the kitchen-porch and turned the door-handle; but the door did not yield to his touch.

Startled at finding it locked he rattled the handle violently; then he reflected that Mattie was alone and that it was natural she should barricade herself at nightfall. He stood in the darkness expecting to hear her step. It did not come, and after vainly straining his ears he called out in a voice that shook with joy: "Hello, Matt!"

Silence answered; but in a minute or two he caught a sound on the stairs and saw a line of light about the door-frame, as he had seen it the night before. So strange was the precision with which the incidents of the previous evening were repeating themselves that he half expected, when he heard the key turn, to see his wife before him on the threshold; but the door opened, and Mattie faced him.

She stood just as Zeena had stood, a lifted lamp in her hand, against the black background of the kitchen. She held the light at the same level, and it drew out with the same distinctness her slim young throat and the brown wrist no bigger than a child's. Then, striking upward, it threw a lustrous fleck on her lips, edged her eyes with velvet shade, and laid a milky whiteness above the black curve of her brows.

She wore her usual dress of darkish stuff, and there was no bow at her neck; but through her hair she had run a streak of crimson ribbon. This tribute to the unusual transformed and glorified her. She seemed to Ethan taller, fuller, more womanly in shape and motion. She stood aside, smiling silently, while he entered, and then moved away from him with something soft and flowing in her gait. She set the lamp on the table, and he saw that it was carefully laid for supper, with fresh dough-nuts, stewed blueberries and his favourite pickles in a dish of gay red glass. A bright fire glowed in the stove and the cat lay stretched before it, watching the table with a drowsy eye.

Ethan was suffocated with the sense of well-being. He went out into the passage to hang up his coat and pull off his wet boots. When he came back Mattie had set the teapot on the table and the cat was rubbing itself persuasively against her ankles.

"Why, Puss! I nearly tripped over you," she cried, the laughter sparkling through her lashes.

Again Ethan felt a sudden twinge of jealousy. Could it be his coming that gave her such a kindled face?

"Well, Matt, any visitors?" he threw off, stooping down carelessly to examine the fastening of the stove.

She nodded and laughed "Yes, one," and he felt a blackness settling on his brows.

"Who was that?" he questioned, raising himself up to slant a glance at her beneath his scowl.

Her eyes danced with malice. "Why, Jotham Powell. He came in after he got back, and asked for a drop of coffee before he went down home."

The blackness lifted and light flooded Ethan's brain. "That all? Well, I hope you made out to let him have it." And after a pause he felt it right to add: "I suppose he got Zeena over to the Flats all right?"

"Oh, yes; in plenty of time."

The name threw a chill between them, and they stood a moment looking sideways at each other before Mattie said with a shy laugh: "I guess it's about time for supper."

They drew their seats up to the table, and the cat, unbidden, jumped between them into Zeena's empty chair. "Oh, Puss!" said Mattie, and they laughed again.

Ethan, a moment earlier, had felt himself on the brink of eloquence; but the mention of Zeena had paralysed him. Mattie seemed to feel the contagion of his embarrassment, and sat with downcast lids, sipping her tea, while he feigned an insatiable appetite for dough-nuts and sweet pickles. At last, after casting about for an effective opening, he took a long gulp of tea, cleared his throat, and said: "Looks as if there'd be more snow."

She feigned great interest. "Is that so? Do you suppose it'll interfere with Zeena's getting back?" She flushed red as the question escaped her, and hastily set down the cup she was lifting.

Ethan reached over for another helping of pickles. "You never can tell, this time of year, it drifts so bad on the Flats." The name had benumbed him again, and once more he felt as if Zeena were in the room between them.

"Oh, Puss, you're too greedy!" Mattie cried.

The cat, unnoticed, had crept up on muffled paws from Zeena's seat to the table, and was stealthily elongating its body in the direction of the milk-jug, which stood between Ethan and Mattie. The two leaned forward at the same moment and their hands met on the handle of the jug. Mattie's hand was underneath, and Ethan kept his clasped on it a moment longer than was necessary. The cat, profiting by this unusual demonstration, tried to effect an unnoticed retreat, and in doing so backed into the pickle-dish, which fell to the floor with a crash.

Mattie, in an instant, had sprung from her chair and was down on her knees by the fragments.

"Oh, Ethan, Ethan—it's all to pieces! What will Zeena say?"

But this time his courage was up. "Well, she'll have to say it to the cat, any way!" he rejoined with a laugh, kneeling down at Mattie's side to scrape up the swimming pickles.

She lifted stricken eyes to him. "Yes, but, you see, she never meant it should be used, not even when there was company; and I had to get up on the step-ladder to reach it down from the top shelf of the china-closet, where she keeps it with all her best things, and of course she'll want to know why I did it——"

The case was so serious that it called forth all of Ethan's latent resolution.

"She needn't know anything about it if you keep quiet. I'll get another just like it to-morrow. Where did it come from? I'll go to Shadd's Falls for it if I have to!"

"Oh, you'll never get another even there! It was a wedding present—don't you remember? It came all the way from Philadelphia, from Zeena's aunt that married the minister. That's why she wouldn't ever use it. Oh, Ethan, Ethan, what in the world shall I do?"

She began to cry, and he felt as if every one of her tears were pouring over him like burning lead. "Don't, Matt, don't—oh, don't!" he implored her.

She struggled to her feet, and he rose and followed her helplessly while she spread out the pieces of glass on the kitchen dresser. It seemed to him as if the shattered fragments of their evening lay there.

"Here, give them to me," he said in a voice of sudden authority.

She drew aside, instinctively obeying his tone. "Oh, Ethan, what are you going to do?"

Without replying he gathered the pieces of glass into his broad palm and walked out of the kitchen to the passage. There he lit a candle-end, opened the china-closet, and, reaching his long arm up to the highest shelf, laid the pieces together with such accuracy

of touch that a close inspection convinced him of the impossibility of detecting from below that the dish was broken. If he glued it
together the next morning months might elapse before his wife
noticed what had happened, and meanwhile he might after all be
able to match the dish at Shadd's Falls or Bettsbridge. Having satisfied himself that there was no risk of immediate discovery he went
back to the kitchen with a lighter step, and found Mattie discon-
solately removing the last scraps of pickle from the floor.

"It's all right, Matt. Come back and finish supper," he commanded her.

Completely reassured, she shone on him through tear-hung
lashes, and his soul swelled with pride as he saw how his tone
subdued her. She did not even ask what he had done. Except
when he was steering a big log down the mountain to his mill he
had never known such a thrilling sense of mastery.

CHAPTER 5

They finished supper, and while Mattie cleared the table Ethan
went to look at the cows and then took a last turn about the
house. The earth lay dark under a muffled sky and the air was so
still that now and then he heard a lump of snow come thumping
down from a tree far off on the edge of the wood-lot.

When he returned to the kitchen Mattie had pushed up his
chair to the stove and seated herself near the lamp with a bit of
sewing. The scene was just as he had dreamed of it that morning.
He sat down, drew his pipe from his pocket and stretched his feet
to the glow. His hard day's work in the keen air made him feel at
once lazy and light of mood, and he had a confused sense of
being in another world, where all was warmth and harmony and
time could bring no change. The only draw-back to his complete
well-being was the fact that he could not see Mattie from where
he sat; but he was too indolent to move and after a moment he
said: "Come over here and sit by the stove."

Zeena's empty rocking-chair stood facing him. Mattie rose obe-diently, and seated herself in it. As her young brown head detached itself against the patch-work cushion that habitually framed his wife's gaunt countenance, Ethan had a momentary shock. It was almost as if the other face, the face of the superseded woman, had obliterated that of the intruder. After a moment Mattie seemed to be affected by the same sense of constraint. She changed her posi-tion, leaning forward to bend her head above her work, so that he saw only the foreshortened tip of her nose and the streak of red in her hair; then she slipped to her feet, saying "I can't see to sew," and went back to her chair by the lamp.

Ethan made a pretext of getting up to replenish the stove, and when he returned to his seat he pushed it sideways that he might get a view of her profile and of the lamplight falling on her hands. The cat, who had been a puzzled observer of these unusual move-ments, jumped up into Zeena's chair, rolled itself into a ball, and lay watching them with narrowed eyes.

Deep quiet sank on the room. The clock ticked above the dresser, a piece of charred wood fell now and then in the stove, and the faint sharp scent of the geraniums mingled with the odour of Ethan's smoke, which began to throw a blue haze about the lamp and to hang its greyish cobwebs in the shadowy corners of the room.

All constraint had vanished between the two, and they began to talk easily and simply. They spoke of every-day things, of the prospect of snow, of the next church sociable, of the loves and quarrels of Starkfield. The commonplace nature of what they said produced in Ethan an illusion of long-established intimacy which no outburst of emotion could have given, and he set his imagina-tion adrift on the fiction that they had always spent their evenings thus and would always go on doing so . . .

"This is the night we were to have gone coasting, Matt," he said at length, with the rich sense, as he spoke, that they could go on any other night they chose, since they had all time before them.

She smiled back at him. "I guess you forgot!"

"No, I didn't forget; but it's as dark as Egypt outdoors. We might go to-morrow if there's a moon."

She laughed with pleasure, her head tilted back, the lamplight sparkling on her lips and teeth. "That would be lovely, Ethan!"

He kept his eyes fixed on her, marvelling at the way her face changed with each turn of their talk, like a wheat-field under a summer breeze. It was intoxicating to find such magic in his clumsy words, and he longed to try new ways of using it.

"Would you be scared to go down the Corbury road with me on a night like this?" he asked.

Her cheeks burned redder. "I ain't any more scared than you are!"

"Well, I'd be scared, then; I wouldn't do it. That's an ugly corner down by the big elm. If a fellow didn't keep his eyes open he'd go plumb into it." He luxuriated in the sense of protection and authority which his words conveyed. To prolong and intensify the feeling he added: "I guess we're well enough here."

She let her lids sink slowly, in the way he loved. "Yes, we're well enough here," she sighed.

Her tone was so sweet that he took the pipe from his mouth and drew his chair up to the table. Leaning forward, he touched the farther end of the strip of brown stuff that she was hemming. "Say, Matt," he began with a smile, "what do you think I saw under the Varnum spruces, coming along home just now? I saw a friend of yours getting kissed."

The words had been on his tongue all the evening, but now that he had spoken them they struck him as inexpressibly vulgar and out of place.

Mattie blushed to the roots of her hair and pulled her needle rapidly twice or thrice through her work, insensibly drawing the end of it away from him. "I suppose it was Ruth and Ned," she said in a low voice, as though he had suddenly touched on something grave.

Ethan had imagined that his allusion might open the way to the accepted pleasantries, and these perhaps in turn to a harmless caress, if only a mere touch on her hand. But now he felt as if her blush had set a flaming guard about her. He supposed it was his natural awkwardness that made him feel so. He knew that most young men made nothing at all of giving a pretty girl a kiss, and he remembered that the night before, when he had put his arm about Mattie, she had not resisted. But that had been out-of-doors, under the open irresponsible night. Now, in the warm lamplit room, with all its ancient implications of conformity and order, she seemed infinitely farther away from him and more unapproachable.

To ease his constraint he said: "I suppose they'll be setting a date before long."

"Yes. I shouldn't wonder if they got married some time along in the summer." She pronounced the word *married* as if her voice caressed it. It seemed a rustling covert leading to enchanted glades. A pang shot through Ethan, and he said, twisting away from her in his chair: "It'll be your turn next, I wouldn't wonder."

She laughed a little uncertainly. "Why do you keep on saying that?"

He echoed her laugh. "I guess I do it to get used to the idea."

He drew up to the table again and she sewed on in silence, with dropped lashes, while he sat in fascinated contemplation of the way in which her hands went up and down above the strip of stuff, just as he had seen a pair of birds make short perpendicular flights over a nest they were building. At length, without turning her head or lifting her lids, she said in a low tone: "It's not because you think Zeena's got anything against me, is it?"

His former dread started up full-armed at the suggestion. "Why, what do you mean?" he stammered.

She raised distressed eyes to his, her work dropping on the table between them. "I don't know. I thought last night she seemed to have."

"I'd like to know what," he growled.

"Nobody can tell with Zeena." It was the first time they had ever spoken so openly of her attitude toward Mattie, and the repetition of the name seemed to carry it to the farther corners of the room and send it back to them in long repercussions of sound. Mattie waited, as if to give the echo time to drop, and then went on: "She hasn't said anything to *you*?"

He shook his head. "No, not a word."

She tossed the hair back from her forehead with a laugh. "I guess I'm just nervous, then. I'm not going to think about it any more."

"Oh, no—don't let's think about it, Matt!"

The sudden heat of his tone made her colour mount again, not with a rush, but gradually, delicately, like the reflection of a thought stealing slowly across her heart. She sat silent, her hands clasped on her work, and it seemed to him that a warm current flowed toward him along the strip of stuff that still lay unrolled between them. Cautiously he slid his hand palm-downward along the table till his finger-tips touched the end of the stuff. A faint vibration of her lashes seemed to show that she was aware of his gesture, and that it had sent a counter-current back to her; and she let her hands lie motionless on the other end of the strip.

As they sat thus he heard a sound behind him and turned his head. The cat had jumped from Zeena's chair to dart at a mouse in the wainscot, and as a result of the sudden movement the empty chair had set up a spectral rocking.

"She'll be rocking in it herself this time to-morrow," Ethan thought. "I've been in a dream, and this is the only evening we'll ever have together." The return to reality was as painful as the return to consciousness after taking an anæsthetic. His body and brain ached with indescribable weariness, and he could think of nothing to say or to do that should arrest the mad flight of the moments.

His alteration of mood seemed to have communicated itself to Mattie. She looked up at him languidly, as though her lids were weighted with sleep and it cost her an effort to raise them. Her glance fell on his hand, which now completely covered the end of her work and grasped it as if it were a part of herself. He saw a scarcely perceptible tremor cross her face, and without knowing what he did he stooped his head and kissed the bit of stuff in his hold. As his lips rested on it he felt it glide slowly from beneath them, and saw that Mattie had risen and was silently rolling up her work. She fastened it with a pin, and then, finding her thimble and scissors, put them with the roll of stuff into the box covered with fancy paper which he had once brought to her from Bettsbridge.

He stood up also, looking vaguely about the room. The clock above the dresser struck eleven.

"Is the fire all right?" she asked in a low voice.

He opened the door of the stove and poked aimlessly at the embers. When he raised himself again he saw that she was dragging toward the stove the old soap-box lined with carpet in which the cat made its bed. Then she recrossed the floor and lifted two of the geranium pots in her arms, moving them away from the cold window. He followed her and brought the other geraniums, the hyacinth bulbs in a cracked custard bowl and the German ivy trained over an old croquet hoop.

When these nightly duties were performed there was nothing left to do but to bring in the tin candlestick from the passage, light the candle and blow out the lamp. Ethan put the candlestick in Mattie's hand and she went out of the kitchen ahead of him, the light that she carried before her making her dark hair look like a drift of mist on the moon.

"Good night, Matt," he said as she put her foot on the first step of the stairs.

She turned and looked at him a moment. "Good night, Ethan," she answered, and went up.

When the door of her room had closed on her he remembered that he had not even touched her hand.

CHAPTER 6

The next morning at breakfast Jotham Powell was between them, and Ethan tried to hide his joy under an air of exaggerated indifference, lounging back in his chair to throw scraps to the cat, growling at the weather, and not so much as offering to help Mattie when she rose to clear away the dishes.

He did not know why he was so irrationally happy, for nothing was changed in his life or hers. He had not even touched the tip of her fingers or looked her full in the eyes. But their evening together had given him a vision of what life at her side might be, and he was glad now that he had done nothing to trouble the sweetness of the picture. He had a fancy that she knew what had restrained him . . .

There was a last load of lumber to be hauled to the village, and Jotham Powell—who did not work regularly for Ethan in winter—had "come round" to help with the job. But a wet snow, melting to sleet, had fallen in the night and turned the roads to glass. There was more wet in the air and it seemed likely to both men that the weather would "milden" toward afternoon and make the going safer. Ethan therefore proposed to his assistant that they should load the sledge at the wood-lot, as they had done on the previous morning, and put off the "teaming" to Starkfield till later in the day. This plan had the advantage of enabling him to send Jotham to the Flats after dinner to meet Zenobia, while he himself took the lumber down to the village.

He told Jotham to go out and harness up the grays, and for a moment he and Mattie had the kitchen to themselves. She had plunged the breakfast dishes into a tin dish-pan and was bending above it with her slim arms bared to the elbow, the steam from the hot water beading her forehead and tightening her rough hair into little brown rings like the tendrils on the traveller's joy.

Ethan stood looking at her, his heart in his throat. He wanted to say: "We shall never be alone again like this." Instead, he reached down his tobacco-pouch from a shelf of the dresser, put it into his pocket and said: "I guess I can make out to be home for dinner."

She answered "All right, Ethan," and he heard her singing over the dishes as he went.

As soon as the sledge was loaded he meant to send Jotham back to the farm and hurry on foot into the village to buy the glue for the pickle-dish. With ordinary luck he should have had time to carry

out this plan; but everything went wrong from the start. On the
way over to the wood-lot one of the grays slipped on a glare of ice
and cut his knee; and when they got him up again Jotham had to
go back to the barn for a strip of rag to bind the cut. Then, when
the loading finally began, a sleety rain was coming down once
more, and the tree trunks were so slippery that it took twice as long
as usual to lift them and get them in place on the sledge. It was
what Jotham called a sour morning for work, and the horses, shiv-
ering and stamping under their wet blankets, seemed to like it as
little as the men. It was long past the dinner-hour when the job was
done, and Ethan had to give up going to the village because he
wanted to lead the injured horse home and wash the cut himself.

He thought that by starting out again with the lumber as soon
as he had finished his dinner he might get back to the farm with
the glue before Jotham and the old sorrel had had time to fetch
Zenobia from the Flats; but he knew the chance was a slight one.
It turned on the state of the roads and on the possible lateness of
the Bettsbridge train. He remembered afterward, with a grim flash
of self-derision, what importance he had attached to the weighing
of these probabilities . . .

As soon as dinner was over he set out again for the wood-lot,
not daring to linger till Jotham Powell left. The hired man was still
drying his wet feet at the stove, and Ethan could only give Mattie
a quick look as he said beneath his breath: "I'll be back early."

He fancied that she nodded her comprehension; and with that
scant solace he had to trudge off through the rain.

He had driven his load half-way to the village when Jotham
Powell overtook him, urging the reluctant sorrel toward the Flats.
"I'll have to hurry up to do it," Ethan mused, as the sleigh
dropped down ahead of him over the dip of the school-house hill.
He worked like ten at the unloading, and when it was over has-
tened on to Michael Eady's for the glue. Eady and his assistant
were both "down street," and young Denis, who seldom deigned
to take their place, was lounging by the stove with a knot of
the golden youth of Starkfield. They hailed Ethan with ironic

compliment and offers of conviviality; but no one knew where to find the glue. Ethan, consumed with the longing for a last moment alone with Mattie, hung about impatiently while Denis made an ineffectual search in the obscurer corners of the store.

"Looks as if we were all sold out. But if you'll wait around till the old man comes along maybe he can put his hand on it."

"I'm obliged to you, but I'll try if I can get it down at Mrs. Homan's," Ethan answered, burning to be gone.

Denis's commercial instinct compelled him to aver on oath that what Eady's store could not produce would never be found at the widow Homan's; but Ethan, heedless of this boast, had already climbed to the sledge and was driving on to the rival establishment. Here, after considerable search, and sympathetic questions as to what he wanted it for, and whether ordinary flour paste wouldn't do as well if she couldn't find it, the widow Homan finally hunted down her solitary bottle of glue to its hiding-place in a medley of cough-lozenges and corset-laces.

"I hope Zeena ain't broken anything she sets store by," she called after him as he turned the grays toward home.

The fitful bursts of sleet had changed into a steady rain and the horses had heavy work even without a load behind them. Once or twice, hearing sleigh-bells, Ethan turned his head, fancying that Zeena and Jotham might overtake him; but the old sorrel was not in sight, and he set his face against the rain and urged on his ponderous pair.

The barn was empty when the horses turned into it and, after giving them the most perfunctory ministrations they had ever received from him, he strode up to the house and pushed open the kitchen door.

Mattie was there alone, as he had pictured her. She was bending over a pan on the stove; but at the sound of his step she turned with a start and sprang to him.

"See, here, Matt, I've got some stuff to mend the dish with! Let me get at it quick," he cried, waving the bottle in one hand while he put her lightly aside; but she did not seem to hear him.

"Oh, Ethan—Zeena's come," she said in a whisper, clutching his sleeve.

They stood and stared at each other, pale as culprits.

"But the sorrel's not in the barn!" Ethan stammered.

"Jotham Powell brought some goods over from the Flats for his wife, and he drove right on home with them," she explained.

He gazed blankly about the kitchen, which looked cold and squalid in the rainy winter twilight.

"How is she?" he asked, dropping his voice to Mattie's whisper.

She looked away from him uncertainly. "I don't know. She went right up to her room."

"She didn't say anything?"

"No."

Ethan let out his doubts in a low whistle and thrust the bottle back into his pocket. "Don't fret; I'll come down and mend it in the night," he said. He pulled on his wet coat again and went back to the barn to feed the grays.

While he was there Jotham Powell drove up with the sleigh, and when the horses had been attended to Ethan said to him: "You might as well come back up for a bite." He was not sorry to assure himself of Jotham's neutralising presence at the supper table, for Zeena was always "nervous" after a journey. But the hired man, though seldom loth to accept a meal not included in his wages, opened his stiff jaws to answer slowly: "I'm obliged to you, but I guess I'll go along back."

Ethan looked at him in surprise. "Better come up and dry off. Looks as if there'd be something hot for supper."

Jotham's facial muscles were unmoved by this appeal and, his vocabulary being limited, he merely repeated: "I guess I'll go along back."

To Ethan there was something vaguely ominous in this stolid rejection of free food and warmth, and he wondered what had happened on the drive to nerve Jotham to such stoicism. Perhaps Zeena had failed to see the new doctor or had not liked his counsels: Ethan knew that in such cases the first person she met was likely to be held responsible for her grievance.

When he re-entered the kitchen the lamp lit up the same scene of shining comfort as on the previous evening. The table had been as carefully laid, a clear fire glowed in the stove, the cat dozed in its warmth, and Mattie came forward carrying a plate of dough-nuts.

She and Ethan looked at each other in silence; then she said, as she had said the night before: "I guess it's about time for supper."

CHAPTER 7

Ethan went out into the passage to hang up his wet garments. He listened for Zeena's step and, not hearing it, called her name up the stairs. She did not answer, and after a moment's hesitation he went up and opened her door. The room was almost dark, but in the obscurity he saw her sitting by the window, bolt upright, and knew by the rigidity of the outline projected against the pane that she had not taken off her travelling dress.

"Well, Zeena," he ventured from the threshold.

She did not move, and he continued: "Supper's about ready. Ain't you coming?"

She replied: "I don't feel as if I could touch a morsel."

It was the consecrated formula, and he expected it to be followed, as usual, by her rising and going down to supper. But she remained seated, and he could think of nothing more felicitous than: "I presume you're tired after the long ride."

Turning her head at this, she answered solemnly: "I'm a great deal sicker than you think."

Her words fell on his ear with a strange shock of wonder. He had often heard her pronounce them before—what if at last they were true?

He advanced a step or two into the dim room. "I hope that's not so, Zeena," he said.

She continued to gaze at him through the twilight with a mien of wan authority, as of one consciously singled out for a great fate. "I've got complications," she said.

Ethan knew the word for one of exceptional import. Almost everybody in the neighbourhood had 'troubles,' frankly localized and specified; but only the chosen had 'complications.' To have them was in itself a distinction, though it was also, in most cases, a death-warrant. People struggled on for years with 'troubles,' but they almost always succumbed to 'complications.'

Ethan's heart was jerking to and fro between two extremities of feeling, but for the moment compassion prevailed. His wife looked so hard and lonely, sitting there in the darkness with such thoughts.

"Is that what the new doctor told you?" he asked, instinctively lowering his voice.

"Yes. He says any regular doctor would want me to have an operation."

Ethan was aware that, in regard to the important question of surgical intervention, the female opinion of the neighbourhood was divided, some glorying in the prestige conferred by operations while others shunned them as indelicate. Ethan, from motives of economy, had always been glad that Zeena was of the latter faction.

In the agitation caused by the gravity of her announcement he sought a consolatory short cut. "What do you know about this doctor anyway? Nobody ever told you that before."

He saw his blunder before she could take it up: she wanted sympathy, not consolation.

"I didn't need to have anybody tell me I was losing ground every day. Everybody but you could see it. And everybody in Bettsbridge knows about Dr. Buck. He has his office in Worcester, and comes over once a fortnight to Shadd's Falls and Bettsbridge for consultations. Eliza Spears was wasting away with kidney trouble before she went to him, and now she's up and around, and singing in the choir."

"Well, I'm glad of that. You must do just what he tells you," Ethan answered sympathetically.

She was still looking at him. "I mean to," she said. He was

struck by a new note in her voice. It was neither whining nor reproachful, but drily resolute.

"What does he want you should do?" he asked, with a mounting vision of fresh expenses.

"He wants I should have a hired girl. He says I oughtn't to have to do a single thing around the house."

"A hired girl?" Ethan stood transfixed.

"Yes. And Aunt Martha found me one right off. Everybody said I was lucky to get a girl to come away out here, and I agreed to give her a dollar extry to make sure. She'll be over to-morrow afternoon."

Wrath and dismay contended in Ethan. He had foreseen an immediate demand for money, but not a permanent drain on his scant resources. He no longer believed what Zeena had told him of the supposed seriousness of her state: he saw in her expedition to Bettsbridge only a plot hatched between herself and her Pierce relations to foist on him the cost of a servant; and for the moment wrath predominated.

"If you meant to engage a girl you ought to have told me before you started," he said.

"How could I tell you before I started? How did I know what Dr. Buck would say?"

"Oh, Dr. Buck—" Ethan's incredulity escaped in a short laugh. "Did Dr. Buck tell you how I was to pay her wages?"

Her voice rose furiously with his. "No, he didn't. For I'd 'a' been ashamed to tell *him* that you grudged me the money to get back my health, when I lost it nursing your own mother!"

"*You* lost your health nursing mother?"

"Yes; and my folks all told me at the time you couldn't do no less than marry me after——"

"Zeena!"

Through the obscurity which hid their faces their thoughts seemed to dart at each other like serpents shooting venom. Ethan was seized with horror of the scene and shame at his own share in it. It was as senseless and savage as a physical fight between two enemies in the darkness.

He turned to the shelf above the chimney, groped for matches and lit the one candle in the room. At first its weak flame made no impression on the shadows; then Zeena's face stood grimly out against the uncurtained pane, which had turned from gray to black.

It was the first scene of open anger between the couple in their sad seven years together, and Ethan felt as if he had lost an irretrievable advantage in descending to the level of recrimination. But the practical problem was there and had to be dealt with.

"You know I haven't got the money to pay for a girl, Zeena. You'll have to send her back: I can't do it."

"The doctor says it'll be my death if I go on slaving the way I've had to. He doesn't understand how I've stood it as long as I have."

"Slaving!—" He checked himself again, "You sha'n't lift a hand, if he says so. I'll do everything round the house myself——"

She broke in: "You're neglecting the farm enough already," and this being true, he found no answer, and left her time to add ironically: "Better send me over to the almshouse and done with it. . . I guess there's been Fromes there afore now."

The taunt burned into him, but he let it pass. "I haven't got the money. That settles it."

There was a moment's pause in the struggle, as though the combatants were testing their weapons. Then Zeena said in a level voice: "I thought you were to get fifty dollars from Andrew Hale for that lumber."

"Andrew Hale never pays under three months." He had hardly spoken when he remembered the excuse he had made for not accompanying his wife to the station the day before; and the blood rose to his frowning brows.

"Why, you told me yesterday you'd fixed it up with him to pay cash down. You said that was why you couldn't drive me over to the Flats."

Ethan had no suppleness in deceiving. He had never before been convicted of a lie, and all the resources of evasion failed him. "I guess that was a misunderstanding," he stammered.

"You ain't got the money?"

"No."

"And you ain't going to get it?"

"No."

"Well, I couldn't know that when I engaged the girl, could I?"

"No." He paused to control his voice. "But you know it now. I'm sorry, but it can't be helped. You're a poor man's wife, Zeena; but I'll do the best I can for you."

For a while she sat motionless, as if reflecting, her arms stretched along the arms of her chair, her eyes fixed on vacancy. "Oh, I guess we'll make out," she said mildly.

The change in her tone reassured him. "Of course we will! There's a whole lot more I can do for you, and Mattie——"

Zeena, while he spoke, seemed to be following out some elaborate mental calculation. She emerged from it to say: "There'll be Mattie's board less, anyhow——"

Ethan, supposing the discussion to be over, had turned to go down to supper. He stopped short, not grasping what he heard. "Mattie's board less—?" he began.

Zeena laughed. It was an odd unfamiliar sound—he did not remember ever having heard her laugh before. "You didn't suppose I was going to keep two girls, did you? No wonder you were scared at the expense!"

He still had but a confused sense of what she was saying. From the beginning of the discussion he had instinctively avoided the mention of Mattie's name, fearing he hardly knew what: criticism, complaints, or vague allusions to the imminent probability of her marrying. But the thought of a definite rupture had never come to him, and even now could not lodge itself in his mind.

"I don't know what you mean," he said. "Mattie Silver's not a hired girl. She's your relation."

"She's a pauper that's hung onto us all after her father'd done his best to ruin us. I've kep' her here a whole year: it's somebody else's turn now."

As the shrill words shot out Ethan heard a tap on the door, which he had drawn shut when he turned back from the threshold.

"Ethan—Zeena!" Mattie's voice sounded gaily from the landing, "do you know what time it is? Supper's been ready half an hour."

Inside the room there was a moment's silence; then Zeena called out from her seat: "I'm not coming down to supper."

"Oh, I'm sorry! Aren't you well? Sha'n't I bring you up a bite of something?"

Ethan roused himself with an effort and opened the door. "Go along down, Matt. Zeena's just a little tired. I'm coming."

He heard her "All right!" and her quick step on the stairs; then he shut the door and turned back into the room. His wife's attitude was unchanged, her face inexorable, and he was seized with the despairing sense of his helplessness.

"You ain't going to do it, Zeena?"

"Do what?" she emitted between flattened lips.

"Send Mattie away—like this?"

"I never bargained to take her for life!"

He continued with rising vehemence: "You can't put her out of the house like a thief—a poor girl without friends or money. She's done her best for you and she's got no place to go to. You may forget she's your kin but everybody else'll remember it. If you do a thing like that what do you suppose folks'll say of you?"

Zeena waited a moment, as if giving him time to feel the full force of the contrast between his own excitement and her composure. Then she replied in the same smooth voice: "I know well enough what they say of my having kep' her here as long as I have."

Ethan's hand dropped from the door-knob, which he had held clenched since he had drawn the door shut on Mattie. His wife's retort was like a knife-cut across the sinews and he felt suddenly weak and powerless. He had meant to humble himself, to argue that Mattie's keep didn't cost much, after all, that he could make out to buy a stove and fix up a place in the attic for the hired girl—but Zeena's words revealed the peril of such pleadings.

"You mean to tell her she's got to go—at once?" he faltered out, in terror of letting his wife complete her sentence.

As if trying to make him see reason she replied impartially; "The girl will be over from Bettsbridge to-morrow, and I presume she's got to have somewheres to sleep."

Ethan looked at her with loathing. She was no longer the listless creature who had lived at his side in a state of sullen self-absorption, but a mysterious alien presence, an evil energy secreted from the long years of silent brooding. It was the sense of his helplessness that sharpened his antipathy. There had never been anything in her that one could appeal to; but as long as he could ignore and command he had remained indifferent. Now she had mastered him and he abhorred her. Mattie was her relation, not his: there were no means by which he could compel her to keep the girl under her roof. All the long misery of his baffled past, of his youth of failure, hardship and vain effort, rose up in his soul in bitterness and seemed to take shape before him in the woman who at every turn had barred his way. She had taken everything else from him; and now she meant to take the one thing that made up for all the others. For a moment such a flame of hate rose in him that it ran down his arm and clenched his fist against her. He took a wild step forward and then stopped.

"You're—you're not coming down?" he said in a bewildered voice.

"No. I guess I'll lay down on the bed a little while," she answered mildly; and he turned and walked out of the room.

In the kitchen Mattie was sitting by the stove, the cat curled up on her knees. She sprang to her feet as Ethan entered and carried the covered dish of meat-pie to the table.

"I hope Zeena isn't sick?" she asked.

"No."

She shone at him across the table. "Well, sit right down then. You must be starving." She uncovered the pie and pushed it over to him. So they were to have one more evening together, her happy eyes seemed to say!

He helped himself mechanically and began to eat; then disgust took him by the throat and he laid down his fork.

Mattie's tender gaze was on him and she marked the gesture.

"Why, Ethan, what's the matter? Don't it taste right?"

"Yes—it's first-rate. Only I—" He pushed his plate away, rose from his chair, and walked around the table to her side. She started up with frightened eyes.

"Ethan, there's something wrong! I *knew* there was!"

She seemed to melt against him in her terror, and he caught her in his arms, held her fast there, felt her lashes beat his cheek like netted butterflies.

"What is it—what is it?" she stammered; but he had found her lips at last and was drinking unconsciousness of everything but the joy they gave him.

She lingered a moment, caught in the same strong current; then she slipped from him and drew back a step or two, pale and troubled. Her look smote him with compunction, and he cried out, as if he saw her drowning in a dream: "You can't go, Matt! I'll never let you!"

"Go—go?" she stammered. "Must I go?"

The words went on sounding between them as though a torch of warning flew from hand to hand through a black landscape.

Ethan was overcome with shame at his lack of self-control in flinging the news at her so brutally. His head reeled and he had to support himself against the table. All the while he felt as if he were still kissing her, and yet dying of thirst for her lips.

"Ethan what has happened? Is Zeena mad with me?"

Her cry steadied him, though it deepened his wrath and pity. "No, no," he assured her, "it's not that. But this new doctor has scared her about herself. You know she believes all they say the first time she sees them. And this one's told her she won't get well unless she lays up and don't do a thing about the house—not for months——"

He paused, his eyes wandering from her miserably. She stood silent a moment, drooping before him like a broken branch. She was so small and weak-looking that it wrung his heart; but suddenly she lifted her head and looked straight at him. "And she wants somebody handier in my place? Is that it?"

"That's what she says to-night."

"If she says it to-night she'll say it to-morrow."

Both bowed to the inexorable truth: they knew that Zeena never changed her mind, and that in her case a resolve once taken was equivalent to an act performed.

There was a long silence between them; then Mattie said in a low voice: "Don't be too sorry, Ethan."

"Oh, God—oh, God," he groaned. The glow of passion he had felt for her had melted to an aching tenderness. He saw her quick lids beating back the tears, and longed to take her in his arms and soothe her.

"You're letting your supper get cold," she admonished him with a pale gleam of gaiety.

"Oh, Matt—Matt—where'll you go to?"

Her lids sank and a tremor crossed her face. He saw that for the first time the thought of the future came to her distinctly. "I might get something to do over at Stamford," she faltered, as if knowing that he knew she had no hope.

He dropped back into his seat and hid his face in his hands. Despair seized him at the thought of her setting out alone to renew the weary quest for work. In the only place where she was known she was surrounded by indifference or animosity; and what chance had she, inexperienced and untrained, among the million bread-seekers of the cities? There came back to him miserable tales he had heard at Worcester, and the faces of girls whose lives had begun as hopefully as Mattie's. . . . It was not possible to think of such things without a revolt of his whole being. He sprang up suddenly.

"You can't go, Matt! I won't let you! She's always had her way, but I mean to have mine now———"

Mattie lifted her hand with a quick gesture, and he heard his wife's step behind him.

Zeena came into the room with her dragging down-at-the-heel step, and quietly took her accustomed seat between them.

"I felt a little mite better, and Dr. Buck says I ought to eat all I can to keep my stren'th up, even if I ain't got any appetite," she said in her flat whine, reaching across Mattie for the teapot. Her "good" dress had been replaced by the black calico and brown knitted shawl which formed her daily wear, and with them she had put on her usual face and manner. She poured out her tea, added a great deal of milk to it, helped herself largely to pie and pickles, and made the familiar gesture of adjusting her false teeth before she began to eat. The cat rubbed itself ingratiatingly against her, and she said "Good Pussy," stooped to stroke it and gave it a scrap of meat from her plate.

Ethan sat speechless, not pretending to eat, but Mattie nibbled valiantly at her food and asked Zeena one or two questions about her visit to Bettsbridge. Zeena answered in her every-day tone and, warming to the theme, regaled them with several vivid descriptions of intestinal disturbances among her friends and relatives. She looked straight at Mattie as she spoke, a faint smile deepening the vertical lines between her nose and chin.

When supper was over she rose from her seat and pressed her hand to the flat surface over the region of her heart. "That pie of yours always sets a mite heavy, Matt," she said, not ill-naturedly. She seldom abbreviated the girl's name, and when she did so it was always a sign of affability.

"I've a good mind to go and hunt up those stomach powders I got last year over in Springfield," she continued. "I ain't tried them for quite a while, and maybe they'll help the heart-burn."

Mattie lifted her eyes. "Can't I get them for you, Zeena?" she ventured.

"No. They're in a place you don't know about," Zeena answered darkly, with one of her secret looks.

She went out of the kitchen and Mattie, rising, began to clear the dishes from the table. As she passed Ethan's chair their eyes met and clung together desolately. The warm still kitchen looked as peaceful as the night before. The cat had sprung to Zeena's rocking-chair, and the heat of the fire was beginning to draw out the faint sharp scent of the geraniums. Ethan dragged himself wearily to his feet.

"I'll go out and take a look round," he said, going toward the passage to get his lantern.

As he reached the door he met Zeena coming back into the room, her lips twitching with anger, a flush of excitement on her sallow face. The shawl had slipped from her shoulders and was dragging at her down-trodden heels, and in her hands she carried the fragments of the red glass pickle-dish.

"I'd like to know who done this," she said, looking sternly from Ethan to Mattie.

There was no answer, and she continued in a trembling voice: "I went to get those powders I'd put away in father's old spectacle-case, top of the china-closet, where I keep the things I set store by, so's folks sha'n't meddle with them—" Her voice broke, and two small tears hung on her lashless lids and ran slowly down her cheeks. "It takes the step-ladder to get at the top shelf, and I put Aunt Philura Maple's pickle-dish up there o' purpose when we was married, and it's never been down since, 'cept for the spring cleaning, and then I always lifted it with my own hands, so's 't it shouldn't get broke." She laid the fragments reverently on the table. "I want to know who done this," she quavered.

At the challenge Ethan turned back into the room and faced her. "I can tell you, then. The cat done it."

"The *cat*?"

"That's what I said."

She looked at him hard, and then turned her eyes to Mattie, who was carrying the dish-pan to the table.

"I'd like to know how the cat got into my china-closet," she said.

"Chasin' mice, I guess," Ethan rejoined. "There was a mouse round the kitchen all last evening."

Zeena continued to look from one to the other; then she emitted her small strange laugh. "I knew the cat was a smart cat," she said in a high voice, "but I didn't know he was smart enough to pick up the pieces of my pickle-dish and lay 'em edge to edge on the very shelf he knocked 'em off of."

Mattie suddenly drew her arms out of the steaming water. "It wasn't Ethan's fault, Zeena! The cat *did* break the dish; but I got it down from the china-closet, and I'm the one to blame for its getting broken."

Zeena stood beside the ruin of her treasure, stiffening into a stony image of resentment. "*You* got down my pickle-dish—what for?"

A bright flush flew to Mattie's cheeks. "I wanted to make the supper-table pretty," she said.

"You wanted to make the supper-table pretty; and you waited till my back was turned, and took the thing I set most store by of anything I've got, and wouldn't never use it, not even when the minister come to dinner, or Aunt Martha Pierce come over from Bettsbridge—" Zeena paused with a gasp, as if terrified by her own evocation of the sacrilege. "You're a bad girl, Mattie Silver, and I always known it. It's the way your father begun, and I was warned of it when I took you, and I tried to keep my things where you couldn't get at 'em—and now you've took from me the one I cared for most of all—" She broke off in a short spasm of sobs that passed and left her more than ever like a shape of stone.

"If I'd 'a' listened to folks, you'd 'a' gone before now, and this wouldn't 'a' happened," she said; and gathering up the bits of broken glass she went out of the room as if she carried a dead body . . .

CHAPTER 8

When Ethan was called back to the farm by his father's illness his mother gave him, for his own use, a small room behind the untenanted "best parlour." Here he had nailed up shelves for his books, built himself a box-sofa out of boards and a mattress, laid out his papers on a kitchen-table, hung on the rough plaster wall an engraving of Abraham Lincoln and a calendar with "Thoughts from the Poets," and tried, with these meagre properties to produce some likeness to the study of a "minister" who had been kind to him and lent him books when he was at Worcester. He still took refuge there in summer, but when Mattie came to live at the farm he had had to give her his stove, and consequently the room was uninhabitable for several months of the year.

To this retreat he descended as soon as the house was quiet, and Zeena's steady breathing from the bed had assured him that there was to be no sequel to the scene in the kitchen. After Zeena's departure he and Mattie had stood speechless, neither seeking to approach the other. Then the girl had returned to her task of clearing up the kitchen for the night and he had taken his lantern and gone on his usual round outside the house. The kitchen was empty when he came back to it; but his tobacco-pouch and pipe had been laid on the table, and under them was a scrap of paper torn from the back of a seedsman's catalogue, on which three words were written: "Don't trouble, Ethan."

Going into his cold dark "study" he placed the lantern on the table and, stooping to its light, read the message again and again. It was the first time that Mattie had ever written to him, and the possession of the paper gave him a strange new sense of her nearness; yet it deepened his anguish by reminding him that henceforth they would have no other way of communicating with each other. For the life of her smile, the warmth of her voice, only cold paper and dead words!

Confused motions of rebellion stormed in him. He was too young, too strong, too full of the sap of living, to submit so easily to the destruction of his hopes. Must he wear out all his years at the side of a bitter querulous woman? Other possibilities had been in him, possibilities sacrificed, one by one, to Zeena's narrow-mindedness and ignorance. And what good had come of it? She was a hundred times bitterer and more discontented than when he had married her: the one pleasure left her was to inflict pain on him. All the healthy instincts of self-defence rose up in him against such waste . . .

He bundled himself into his old coon-skin coat and lay down on the box-sofa to think. Under his cheek he felt a hard object with strange protuberances. It was a cushion which Zeena had made for him when they were engaged—the only piece of needlework he had ever seen her do. He flung it across the floor and propped his head against the wall . . .

He knew a case of a man over the mountain—a young fellow of about his own age—who had escaped from just such a life of misery by going West with the girl he cared for. His wife had divorced him, and he had married the girl and prospered. Ethan had seen the couple the summer before at Shadd's Falls, where they had come to visit relatives. They had a little girl with fair curls, who wore a gold locket and was dressed like a princess. The deserted wife had not done badly either. Her husband had given her the farm and she had managed to sell it, and with that and the alimony she had started a lunch-room at Bettsbridge and bloomed into activity and importance. Ethan was fired by the thought. Why should he not leave with Mattie the next day, instead of letting her go alone? He would hide his valise under the seat of the sleigh, and Zeena would suspect nothing till she went upstairs for her afternoon nap and found a letter on the bed . . .

His impulses were still near the surface, and he sprang up, re-lit the lantern, and sat down at the table. He rummaged in the drawer for a sheet of paper, found one, and began to write.

"Zeena, I've done all I could for you, and I don't see as it's been any use. I don't blame you, nor I don't blame myself. Maybe both of us will do better separate. I'm going to try my luck West, and you can sell the farm and mill, and keep the money—"

His pen paused on the word, which brought home to him the relentless conditions of his lot. If he gave the farm and mill to Zeena what would be left him to start his own life with? Once in the West he was sure of picking up work—he would not have

feared to try his chance alone. But with Mattie depending on him
the case was different. And what of Zeena's fate? Farm and mill
were mortgaged to the limit of their value, and even if she found a
purchaser—in itself an unlikely chance—it was doubtful if she
could clear a thousand dollars on the sale. Meanwhile, how could
she keep the farm going? It was only by incessant labour and personal supervision that Ethan drew a meagre living from his land,
and his wife, even if she were in better health than she imagined,
could never carry such a burden alone.

Well, she could go back to her people, then, and see what they
would do for her. It was the fate she was forcing on Mattie—why
not let her try it herself? By the time she had discovered his
whereabouts, and brought suit for divorce, he would probably—
wherever he was—be earning enough to pay her a sufficient
alimony. And the alternative was to let Mattie go forth alone, with
far less hope of ultimate provision . . .

He had scattered the contents of the table-drawer in his search
for a sheet of paper, and as he took up his pen his eye fell on an
old copy of the *Bettsbridge Eagle*. The advertising sheet was folded
uppermost, and he read the seductive words: "Trips to the West:
Reduced Rates."

He drew the lantern nearer and eagerly scanned the fares; then
the paper fell from his hand and he pushed aside his unfinished
letter. A moment ago he had wondered what he and Mattie were
to live on when they reached the West; now he saw that he had
not even the money to take her there. Borrowing was out of the
question: six months before he had given his only security to raise
funds for necessary repairs to the mill, and he knew that without
security no one at Starkfield would lend him ten dollars. The inexorable facts closed in on him like prison-warders hand-cuffing
a convict. There was no way out—none. He was a prisoner for
life, and now his one ray of light was to be extinguished.

He crept back heavily to the sofa, stretching himself out with
limbs so leaden that he felt as if they would never move again.
Tears rose in his throat and slowly burned their way to his lids.

As he lay there, the window-pane that faced him, growing gradually lighter, inlaid upon the darkness a square of moon-suffused sky. A crooked tree-branch crossed it, a branch of the apple-tree under which, on summer evenings, he had sometimes found Mattie sitting when he came up from the mill. Slowly the rim of the rainy vapours caught fire and burnt away, and a pure moon swung into the blue. Ethan, rising on his elbow, watched the landscape whiten and shape itself under the sculpture of the moon. This was the night on which he was to have taken Mattie coasting, and there hung the lamp to light them! He looked out at the slopes bathed in lustre, the silver-edged darkness of the woods, the spectral purple of the hills against the sky, and it seemed as though all the beauty of the night had been poured out to mock his wretchedness . . .

He fell asleep, and when he woke the chill of the winter dawn was in the room. He felt cold and stiff and hungry, and ashamed of being hungry. He rubbed his eyes and went to the window. A red sun stood over the gray rim of the fields, behind trees that looked black and brittle. He said to himself: "This is Matt's last day," and tried to think what the place would be without her.

As he stood there he heard a step behind him and she entered.

"Oh, Ethan—were you here all night?"

She looked so small and pinched, in her poor dress, with the red scarf wound about her, and the cold light turning her paleness sallow, that Ethan stood before her without speaking.

"You must be frozen," she went on, fixing lustreless eyes on him.

He drew a step nearer. "How did you know I was here?"

"Because I heard you go down stairs again after I went to bed, and I listened all night, and you didn't come up."

All his tenderness rushed to his lips. He looked at her and said: "I'll come right along and make up the kitchen fire."

They went back to the kitchen, and he fetched the coal and kindlings and cleared out the stove for her, while she brought in the milk and the cold remains of the meat-pie. When warmth began to radiate from the stove, and the first ray of sunlight lay on the kitchen floor, Ethan's dark thoughts melted in the mellower air. The sight of Mattie going about her work as he had seen her on so many mornings made it seem impossible that she could ever cease to be a part of the scene. He said to himself that he had doubtless exaggerated the significance of Zeena's threats, and that she too, with the return of daylight, would come to a saner mood.

He went up to Mattie as she bent above the stove, and laid his hand on her arm. "I don't want you should trouble either," he said, looking down into her eyes with a smile.

She flushed up warmly and whispered back: "No, Ethan, I ain't going to trouble."

"I guess things'll straighten out," he added.

There was no answer but a quick throb of her lids, and he went on: "She ain't said anything this morning?"

"No. I haven't seen her yet."

"Don't you take any notice when you do."

With this injunction he left her and went out to the cow-barn. He saw Jotham Powell walking up the hill through the morning mist, and the familiar sight added to his growing conviction of security.

As the two men were clearing out the stalls Jotham rested on his pitch-fork to say: "Dan'l Byrne's goin' over to the Flats to-day noon, an' he c'd take Mattie's trunk along, and make it easier ridin' when I take her over in the sleigh."

Ethan looked at him blankly, and he continued: "Mis' Frome said the new girl'd be at the Flats at five, and I was to take Mattie then, so's 't she could ketch the six o'clock train for Stamford."

Ethan felt the blood drumming in his temples. He had to wait a moment before he could find voice to say: "Oh, it ain't so sure about Mattie's going——"

"That so?" said Jotham indifferently; and they went on with their work.

When they returned to the kitchen the two women were already at breakfast. Zeena had an air of unusual alertness and activity. She drank two cups of coffee and fed the cat with the scraps left in the pie-dish; then she rose from her seat and, walking over to the window, snipped two or three yellow leaves from the geraniums. "Aunt Martha's ain't got a faded leaf on 'em; but they pine away when they ain't cared for," she said reflectively. Then she turned to Jotham and asked: "What time'd you say Dan'l Byrne'd be along?"

The hired man threw a hesitating glance at Ethan. "Round about noon," he said.

Zeena turned to Mattie. "That trunk of yours is too heavy for the sleigh, and Dan'l Byrne'll be round to take it over to the Flats," she said.

"I'm much obliged to you, Zeena," said Mattie.

"I'd like to go over things with you first," Zeena continued in an unperturbed voice. "I know there's a huckabuck towel missing; and I can't make out what you done with that match-safe 't used to stand behind the stuffed owl in the parlour."

She went out, followed by Mattie, and when the men were alone Jotham said to his employer: "I guess I better let Dan'l come round, then."

Ethan finished his usual morning tasks about the house and barn; then he said to Jotham: "I'm going down to Starkfield. Tell them not to wait dinner."

The passion of rebellion had broken out in him again. That which had seemed incredible in the sober light of day had really come to pass, and he was to assist as a helpless spectator at Mattie's banishment. His manhood was humbled by the part he was compelled to play and by the thought of what Mattie must think of him. Confused impulses struggled in him as he strode along to the village. He had made up his mind to do something, but he did not know what it would be.

The early mist had vanished and the fields lay like a silver shield under the sun. It was one of the days when the glitter of winter shines through a pale haze of spring. Every yard of the road was alive with Mattie's presence, and there was hardly a branch against the sky or a tangle of brambles on the bank in which some bright shred of memory was not caught. Once, in the stillness, the call of a bird in a mountain ash was so like her laughter that his heart tightened and then grew large; and all these things made him see that something must be done at once.

Suddenly it occurred to him that Andrew Hale, who was a kind-hearted man, might be induced to reconsider his refusal and advance a small sum on the lumber if he were told that Zeena's ill-health made it necessary to hire a servant. Hale, after all, knew enough of Ethan's situation to make it possible for the latter to renew his appeal without too much loss of pride; and, more-over, how much did pride count in the ebullition of passions in his breast?

The more he considered his plan the more hopeful it seemed. If he could get Mrs. Hale's ear he felt certain of success, and with fifty dollars in his pocket nothing could keep him from Mattie . . .

His first object was to reach Starkfield before Hale had started for his work; he knew the carpenter had a job down the Corbury road and was likely to leave his house early. Ethan's long strides grew more rapid with the accelerated beat of his thoughts, and as he reached the foot of School House Hill he caught sight of Hale's sleigh in the distance. He hurried forward to meet it, but as it drew nearer he saw that it was driven by the carpenter's youngest boy and that the figure at his side, looking like a large upright cocoon in spectacles, was that of Mrs. Hale. Ethan signed to them to stop, and Mrs. Hale leaned forward, her pink wrinkles twin-kling with benevolence.

"Mr. Hale? Why, yes, you'll find him down home now. He ain't going to his work this forenoon. He woke up with a touch o' lum-bago, and I just made him put on one of old Dr. Kidder's plasters and set right up into the fire."

Beaming maternally on Ethan, she bent over to add: "I on'y just heard from Mr. Hale 'bout Zeena's going over to Bettsbridge to see that new doctor. I'm real sorry she's feeling so bad again! I hope he thinks he can do something for her? I don't know any-body round here's had more sickness than Zeena. I always tell Mr.

Hale I don't know what she'd 'a' done if she hadn't 'a' had you to look after her; and I used to say the same thing 'bout your mother. You've had an awful mean time, Ethan Frome."

She gave him a last nod of sympathy while her son chirped to the horse; and Ethan, as she drove off, stood in the middle of the road and stared after the retreating sleigh.

It was a long time since any one had spoken to him as kindly as Mrs. Hale. Most people were either indifferent to his troubles, or disposed to think it natural that a young fellow of his age should have carried without repining the burden of three crippled lives. But Mrs. Hale had said "You've had an awful mean time, Ethan Frome," and he felt less alone with his misery. If the Hales were sorry for him they would surely respond to his appeal . . .

He started down the road toward their house, but at the end of a few yards he pulled up sharply, the blood in his face. For the first time, in the light of the words he had just heard, he saw what he was about to do. He was planning to take advantage of the Hales' sympathy to obtain money from them on false pretences. That was a plain statement of the cloudy purpose which had driven him in headlong to Starkfield.

With the sudden perception of the point to which his madness had carried him, the madness fell and he saw his life before him as it was. He was a poor man, the husband of a sickly woman, whom his desertion would leave alone and destitute; and even if he had had the heart to desert her he could have done so only by deceiving two kindly people who had pitied him.

He turned and walked slowly back to the farm.

CHAPTER 9

At the kitchen door Daniel Byrne sat in his sleigh behind a big-boned gray who pawed the snow and swung his long head restlessly from side to side.

Ethan went into the kitchen and found his wife by the stove.

Her head was wrapped in her shawl, and she was reading a book called "Kidney Troubles And Their Cure" on which he had had to pay extra postage only a few days before.

Zeena did not move or look up when he entered, and after a moment he asked: "Where's Mattie?"

Without lifting her eyes from the page she replied: "I presume she's getting down her trunk."

The blood rushed to his face. "Getting down her trunk—alone?"

"Jotham Powell's down in the wood-lot, and Dan'l Byrne says he darsn't leave the horse," she returned.

Her husband, without stopping to hear the end of the phrase, had left the kitchen and sprung up the stairs. The door of Mattie's room was shut, and he wavered a moment on the landing. "Matt," he said in a low voice; but there was no answer, and he put his hand on the door-knob.

He had never been in her room except once, in the early summer, when he had gone there to plaster up a leak in the eaves, but he remembered exactly how everything had looked: the red and white quilt on her narrow bed, the pretty pin-cushion on the chest of drawers, and over it the enlarged photograph of her mother, in an oxydized frame, with a bunch of dyed grasses at the back. Now these and all other tokens of her presence had vanished, and the room looked as bare and comfortless as when Zeena had shown her into it on the day of her arrival. In the middle of the floor stood her trunk, and on the trunk she sat in her Sunday dress, her back turned to the door and her face in her hands. She had not heard Ethan's call because she was sobbing; and she did not hear his step till he stood close behind her and laid his hands on her shoulders.

"Matt—oh, don't—oh, *Matt!*"

She started up, lifting her wet face to his. "Ethan—I thought I wasn't ever going to see you again!"

He took her in his arms, pressing her close, and with a trembling hand smoothed away the hair from her forehead.

"Not see me again? What do you mean?"

She sobbed out: "Jotham said you told him we wasn't to wait dinner for you, and I thought—"

"You thought I meant to cut it?" he finished for her grimly.

She clung to him without answering, and he laid his lips on her hair, which was soft yet springy, like certain mosses on warm slopes, and had the faint woody fragrance of fresh sawdust in the sun.

Through the door they heard Zeena's voice calling out from below: "Dan'l Byrne says you better hurry up if you want him to take that trunk."

They drew apart with stricken faces. Words of resistance rushed to Ethan's lips and died there. Mattie found her handkerchief and dried her eyes; then, bending down, she took hold of a handle of the trunk.

Ethan put her aside. "You let go, Matt," he ordered her.

She answered: "It takes two to coax it round the corner"; and submitting to this argument he grasped the other handle, and together they manœuvred the heavy trunk out to the landing.

"Now let go," he repeated; then he shouldered the trunk and carried it down the stairs and across the passage to the kitchen. Zeena, who had gone back to her seat by the stove, did not lift her head from her book as he passed. Mattie followed him out of the door and helped him to lift the trunk into the back of the sleigh. When it was in place they stood side by side on the door-step, watching Daniel Byrne plunge off behind his fidgety horse.

It seemed to Ethan that his heart was bound with cords which an unseen hand was tightening with every tick of the clock. Twice he opened his lips to speak to Mattie and found no breath. At length, as she turned to re-enter the house, he laid a detaining hand on her.

"I'm going to drive you over, Matt," he whispered.

She murmured back: "I think Zeena wants I should go with Jotham."

"I'm going to drive you over," he repeated; and she went into the kitchen without answering.

At dinner Ethan could not eat. If he lifted his eyes they rested on Zeena's pinched face, and the corners of her straight lips seemed to quiver away into a smile. She ate well, declaring that the mild weather made her feel better, and pressed a second helping of beans on Jotham Powell, whose wants she generally ignored.

Mattie, when the meal was over, went about her usual task of clearing the table and washing up the dishes. Zeena, after feeding the cat, had returned to her rocking-chair by the stove, and Jotham Powell, who always lingered last, reluctantly pushed back his chair and moved toward the door.

On the threshold he turned back to say to Ethan, "What time'll I come round for Mattie?"

Ethan was standing near the window, mechanically filling his pipe while he watched Mattie move to and fro. He answered: "You needn't come round; I'm going to drive her over myself."

He saw the rise of the colour in Mattie's averted cheek, and the quick lifting of Zeena's head.

"I want you should stay here this afternoon, Ethan," his wife said. "Jotham can drive Mattie over."

Mattie flung an imploring glance at him, but he repeated curtly: "I'm going to drive her over myself."

Zeena continued in the same even tone: "I wanted you should stay and fix up that stove in Mattie's room afore the girl gets here. It ain't been drawing right for nigh on a month now."

Ethan's voice rose indignantly. "If it was good enough for Mattie I guess it's good enough for a hired girl."

"That girl that's coming told me she was used to a house where they had a furnace," Zeena persisted with the same monotonous mildness.

"She'd better ha' stayed there then," he flung back at her; and turning to Mattie he added in a hard voice: "You be ready by three, Matt; I've got business at Corbury."

Jotham Powell had started for the barn, and Ethan strode down after him aflame with anger. The pulses in his temples throbbed and a fog was in his eyes. He went about his task without knowing

what force directed him, or whose hands and feet were fulfilling
its orders. It was not till he led out the sorrel and backed him
between the shafts of the sleigh that he once more became conscious of what he was doing. As he passed the bridle over the
horse's head, and wound the traces around the shafts, he remembered the day when he had made the same preparations in order
to drive over and meet his wife's cousin at the Flats. It was little
more than a year ago, on just such a soft afternoon, with a "feel"
of spring in the air. The sorrel, turning the same big ringed eye on
him, nuzzled the palm of his hand in the same way; and one by
one all the days between rose up and stood before him . . .

He flung the bearskin into the sleigh, climbed to the seat, and
drove up to the house. When he entered the kitchen it was empty,
but Mattie's bag and shawl lay ready by the door. He went to the
foot of the stairs and listened. No sound reached him from above,
but presently he thought he heard some one moving about in his
deserted study, and pushing open the door he saw Mattie, in her
hat and jacket, standing with her back to him near the table.

She started at his approach and turning quickly, said: "Is
it time?"

"What are you doing here, Matt?" he asked her.

She looked at him timidly. "I was just taking a look round—
that's all," she answered, with a wavering smile.

They went back into the kitchen without speaking, and Ethan
picked up her bag and shawl.

"Where's Zeena?" he asked.

"She went upstairs right after dinner. She said she had those
shooting pains again, and didn't want to be disturbed."

"Didn't she say good-bye to you?"

"No. That was all she said."

Ethan, looking slowly about the kitchen, said to himself with a
shudder that in a few hours he would be returning to it alone.
Then the sense of unreality overcame him once more, and he
could not bring himself to believe that Mattie stood there for the
last time before him.

"Come on," he said almost gaily, opening the door and putting her bag into the sleigh. He sprang to his seat and bent over to tuck the rug about her as she slipped into the place at his side. "Now then, go 'long," he said, with a shake of the reins that sent the sorrel placidly jogging down the hill.

"We got lots of time for a good ride, Matt!" he cried, seeking her hand beneath the fur and pressing it in his. His face tingled and he felt dizzy, as if he had stopped in at the Starkfield saloon on a zero day for a drink.

At the gate, instead of making for Starkfield, he turned the sorrel to the right, up the Bettsbridge road. Mattie sat silent, giving no sign of surprise; but after a moment she said: "Are you going round by Shadow Pond?"

He laughed and answered: "I knew you'd know!"

She drew closer under the bearskin, so that, looking sideways around his coat-sleeve, he could just catch the tip of her nose and a blown brown wave of hair. They drove slowly up the road between fields glistening under the pale sun, and then bent to the right down a lane edged with spruce and larch. Ahead of them, a long way off, a range of hills stained by mottlings of black forest flowed away in round white curves against the sky. The lane passed into a pine-wood with boles reddening in the afternoon sun and delicate blue shadows on the snow. As they entered it the breeze fell and a warm stillness seemed to drop from the branches with the dropping needles. Here the snow was so pure that the tiny tracks of wood-animals had left on it intricate lace-like patterns, and the bluish cones caught in its surface stood out like ornaments of bronze.

Ethan drove on in silence till they reached a part of the wood where the pines were more widely spaced: then he drew up and helped Mattie to get out of the sleigh. They passed between the aromatic trunks, the snow breaking crisply under their feet, till they came to a small sheet of water with steep wooded sides. Across its frozen surface, from the farther bank, a single hill rising against the western sun threw the long conical shadow which gave the lake its name. It was a shy secret spot, full of the same dumb melancholy that Ethan felt in his heart.

He looked up and down the little pebbly beach till his eye lit on a fallen tree-trunk half submerged in snow.

"There's where we sat at the picnic," he reminded her.

The entertainment of which he spoke was one of the few that they had taken part in together: a "church picnic" which, on a long afternoon of the preceding summer, had filled the retired place with merry-making. Mattie had begged him to go with her but he had refused. Then, toward sunset, coming down from the mountain where he had been felling timber, he had been caught by some strayed revellers and drawn into the group by the lake, where Mattie, encircled by facetious youths, and bright as a black-berry under her spreading hat, was brewing coffee over a gipsy fire. He remembered the shyness he had felt at approaching her in his uncouth clothes, and then the lighting up of her face, and the way she had broken through the group to come to him with a cup in her hand. They had sat for a few minutes on the fallen log by the pond, and she had missed her gold locket, and set the young men searching for it; and it was Ethan who had spied it in the moss . . . That was all; but all their intercourse had been made up of just such inarticulate flashes, when they seemed to come sud-denly upon happiness as if they had surprised a butterfly in the winter woods . . .

"It was right there I found your locket," he said, pushing his foot into a dense tuft of blueberry bushes.

"I never saw anybody with such sharp eyes!" she answered.

She sat down on the tree-trunk in the sun and he sat down beside her.

"You were as pretty as a picture in that pink hat," he said.

She laughed with pleasure. "Oh, I guess it was the hat!" she rejoined.

They had never before avowed their inclination so openly, and Ethan, for a moment, had the illusion that he was a free man, wooing the girl he meant to marry. He looked at her hair and longed to touch it again, and to tell her that it smelt of the woods; but he had never learned to say such things.

Suddenly she rose to her feet and said: "We mustn't stay here any longer."

He continued to gaze at her vaguely, only half-roused from his dream. "There's plenty of time," he answered.

They stood looking at each other as if the eyes of each were straining to absorb and hold fast the other's image. There were things he had to say to her before they parted, but he could not say them in that place of summer memories, and he turned and followed her in silence to the sleigh. As they drove away the sun sank behind the hill and the pine-boles turned from red to gray.

By a devious track between the fields they wound back to the Starkfield road. Under the open sky the light was still clear, with a reflection of cold red on the eastern hills. The clumps of trees in the snow seemed to draw together in ruffled lumps, like birds with their heads under their wings; and the sky, as it paled, rose higher, leaving the earth more alone.

As they turned into Starkfield road Ethan said: "Matt, what do you mean to do?"

She did not answer at once, but at length she said: "I'll try to get a place in a store."

"You know you can't do it. The bad air and the standing all day nearly killed you before."

"I'm a lot stronger than I was before I came to Starkfield."

"And now you're going to throw away all the good it's done you!"

There seemed to be no answer to this, and again they drove on for a while without speaking. With every yard of the way some spot where they had stood, and laughed together or been silent, clutched at Ethan and dragged him back.

"Isn't there any of your father's folks could help you?"

"There isn't any of 'em I'd ask."

He lowered his voice to say: "You know there's nothing I wouldn't do for you if I could."

"I know there isn't."

"But I can't——"

She was silent, but he felt a slight tremor in the shoulder against his.

"Oh, Matt," he broke out, "if I could ha' gone with you now I'd ha' done it——"

She turned to him, pulling a scrap of paper from her breast. "Ethan—I found this," she stammered. Even in the failing light he saw it was the letter to his wife that he had begun the night before and forgotten to destroy. Through his astonishment there ran a fierce thrill of joy. "Matt—" he cried; "if I could ha' done it, would you?"

"Oh, Ethan, Ethan—what's the use?" With a sudden movement she tore the letter in shreds and sent them fluttering off into the snow.

"Tell me, Matt! Tell me!" he adjured her.

She was silent for a moment; then she said, in such a low tone that he had to stoop his head to hear her: "I used to think of it sometimes, summer nights, when the moon was so bright I couldn't sleep."

His heart reeled with the sweetness of it. "As long ago as that?"

She answered, as if the date had long been fixed for her: "The first time was at Shadow Pond."

"Was that why you gave me my coffee before the others?"

"I don't know. Did I? I was dreadfully put out when you wouldn't go to the picnic with me; and then, when I saw you coming down the road, I thought maybe you'd gone home that way o' purpose; and that made me glad."

They were silent again. They had reached the point where the road dipped to the hollow by Ethan's mill and as they descended the darkness descended with them, dropping down like a black veil from the heavy hemlock boughs.

"I'm tied hand and foot, Matt. There isn't a thing I can do," he began again.

"You must write to me sometimes, Ethan."

"Oh, what good'll writing do? I want to put my hand out and touch you. I want to do for you and care for you. I want to be there when you're sick and when you're lonesome."

"You mustn't think but what I'll do all right."

"You won't need me, you mean? I suppose you'll marry!"

"Oh, Ethan!" she cried.

"I don't know how it is you make me feel, Matt. I'd a'most rather have you dead than that!"

"Oh, I wish I was, I wish I was!" she sobbed.

The sound of her weeping shook him out of his dark anger, and he felt ashamed.

"Don't let's talk that way," he whispered.

"Why shouldn't we, when it's true? I've been wishing it every minute of the day."

"Matt! You be quiet! Don't you say it."

"There's never anybody been good to me but you."

"Don't say that either, when I can't lift a hand for you!"

"Yes; but it's true just the same."

They had reached the top of School House Hill and Starkfield lay below them in the twilight. A cutter, mounting the road from the village, passed them by in a joyous flutter of bells, and they straightened themselves and looked ahead with rigid faces. Along the main street lights had begun to shine from the house-fronts and stray figures were turning in here and there at the gates. Ethan, with a touch of his whip, roused the sorrel to a languid trot.

As they drew near the end of the village the cries of children reached them, and they saw a knot of boys, with sleds behind them, scattering across the open space before the church.

"I guess this'll be their last coast for a day or two," Ethan said, looking up at the mild sky.

Mattie was silent, and he added: "We were to have gone down last night."

Still she did not speak and, prompted by an obscure desire to help himself and her through their miserable last hour, he went on discursively: "Ain't it funny we haven't been down together but just that once last winter?"

She answered: "It wasn't often I got down to the village."

"That's so," he said.

They had reached the crest of the Corbury road, and between the indistinct white glimmer of the church and the black curtain of the Varnum spruces the slope stretched away below them without a sled on its length. Some erratic impulse prompted Ethan to say: "How'd you like me to take you down now?"

She forced a laugh. "Why, there isn't time!"

"There's all the time we want. Come along!" His one desire now was to postpone the moment of turning the sorrel toward the Flats.

"But the girl," she faltered. "The girl'll be waiting at the station."

"Well, let her wait. You'd have to if she didn't. Come!"

The note of authority in his voice seemed to subdue her, and when he had jumped from the sleigh she let him help her out, saying only, with a vague feint of reluctance: "But there isn't a sled round any wheres."

"Yes, there is! Right over there under the spruces."

He threw the bearskin over the sorrel, who stood passively by the roadside, hanging a meditative head. Then he caught Mattie's hand and drew her after him toward the sled.

She seated herself obediently and he took his place behind her, so close that her hair brushed his face. "All right, Matt?" he called out, as if the width of the road had been between them.

She turned her head to say: "It's dreadfully dark. Are you sure you can see?"

He laughed contemptuously: "I could go down this coast with my eyes tied!" and she laughed with him, as if she liked his audacity. Nevertheless he sat still a moment, straining his eyes down the long hill, for it was the most confusing hour of the evening, the hour when the last clearness from the upper sky is merged with the rising night in a blur that disguises landmarks and falsifies distances.

"Now!" he cried.

The sled started with a bound, and they flew on through the dusk, gathering smoothness and speed as they went, with the hollow night opening out below them and the air singing by like an organ. Mattie sat perfectly still, but as they reached the bend at the foot of the hill, where the big elm thrust out a deadly elbow, he fancied that she shrank a little closer.

"Don't be scared, Matt!" he cried exultantly, as they spun safely past it and flew down the second slope; and when they reached the level ground beyond, and the speed of the sled began to slacken, he heard her give a little laugh of glee.

They sprang off and started to walk back up the hill. Ethan dragged the sled with one hand and passed the other through Mattie's arm.

"Were you scared I'd run you into the elm?" he asked with a boyish laugh.

"I told you I was never scared with you," she answered.

The strange exaltation of his mood had brought on one of his rare fits of boastfulness. "It *is* a tricky place, though. The least swerve, and we'd never ha' come up again. But I can measure distances to a hair's-breadth—always could."

She murmured: "I always say you've got the surest eye . . ."

Deep silence had fallen with the starless dusk, and they leaned on each other without speaking; but at every step of their climb Ethan said to himself: "It's the last time we'll ever walk together."

They mounted slowly to the top of the hill. When they were abreast of the church he stooped his head to her to ask: "Are you tired?" and she answered, breathing quickly: "It was splendid!"

With a pressure of his arm he guided her toward the Norway spruces. "I guess this sled must be Ned Hale's. Anyhow I'll leave it where I found it." He drew the sled up to the Varnum gate and rested it against the fence. As he raised himself he suddenly felt Mattie close to him among the shadows.

"Is this where Ned and Ruth kissed each other?" she whispered breathlessly, and flung her arms about him. Her lips,

groping for his, swept over his face, and he held her fast in a rapture of surprise.

"Good-bye—good-bye," she stammered, and kissed him again.

"Oh, Matt I can't let you go!" broke from him in the same
old cry.

She freed herself from his hold and he heard her sobbing. "Oh,
I can't go either!" she wailed.

"Matt! What'll we do? What'll we do?"

They clung to each other's hands like children, and her body
shook with desperate sobs.

Through the stillness they heard the church clock striking five.

"Oh, Ethan, it's time!" she cried.

He drew her back to him. "Time for what? You don't suppose
I'm going to leave you now?"

"If I missed my train where'd I go?"

"Where are you going if you catch it?"

She stood silent, her hands lying cold and relaxed in his.

"What's the good of either of us going anywheres without the
other one now?" he said.

She remained motionless, as if she had not heard him. Then
she snatched her hands from his, threw her arms about his neck,
and pressed a sudden drenched cheek against his face. "Ethan!
Ethan! I want you to take me down again!"

"Down where?"

"The coast. Right off," she panted. "So 't we'll never come up
any more."

"Matt! What on earth do you mean?"

She put her lips close against his ear to say: "Right into the big
elm. You said you could. So 't we'd never have to leave each other
any more."

"Why, what are you talking of? You're crazy!"

"I'm not crazy; but I will be if I leave you."

"Oh, Matt, Matt—" he groaned.

She tightened her fierce hold about his neck. Her face lay close
to his face.

"Ethan, where'll I go if I leave you? I don't know how to get along alone. You said so yourself just now. Nobody but you was ever good to me. And there'll be that strange girl in the house . . . and she'll sleep in my bed, where I used to lay nights and listen to hear you come up the stairs. . ."

The words were like fragments torn from his heart. With them came the hated vision of the house he was going back to—of the stairs he would have to go up every night, of the woman who would wait for him there. And the sweetness of Mattie's avowal, the wild wonder of knowing at last that all that had happened to him had happened to her too, made the other vision more abhorrent, the other life more intolerable to return to . . .

Her pleadings still came to him between short sobs, but he no longer heard what she was saying. Her hat had slipped back and he was stroking her hair. He wanted to get the feeling of it into his hand, so that it would sleep there like a seed in winter. Once he found her mouth again, and they seemed to be by the pond together in the burning August sun. But his cheek touched hers, and it was cold and full of weeping, and he saw the road to the Flats under the night and heard the whistle of the train up the line.

The spruces swathed them in blackness and silence. They might have been in their coffins underground. He said to himself: "Perhaps it'll feel like this . . ." and then again: "After this I sha'n't feel anything. . ."

Suddenly he heard the old sorrel whinny across the road, and thought: "He's wondering why he doesn't get his supper. . ."

"Come," Mattie whispered, tugging at his hand.

Her sombre violence constrained him: she seemed the embodied instrument of fate. He pulled the sled out, blinking like a night-bird as he passed from the shade of the spruces into the transparent dusk of the open. The slope below them was deserted. All Starkfield was at supper, and not a figure crossed the open space before the church. The sky, swollen with the clouds that announce a thaw, hung as low as before a summer storm. He strained his eyes through the dimness, and they seemed less keen, less capable than usual.

He took his seat on the sled and Mattie instantly placed herself in front of him. Her hat had fallen into the snow and his lips were in her hair. He stretched out his legs, drove his heels into the road to keep the sled from slipping forward, and bent her head back between his hands. Then suddenly he sprang up again.

"Get up," he ordered her.

It was the tone she always heeded, but she cowered down in her seat, repeating vehemently: "No, no, no!"

"Get up!"

"Why?"

"I want to sit in front."

"No, no! How can you steer in front?"

"I don't have to. We'll follow the track."

They spoke in smothered whispers, as though the night were listening.

"Get up! Get up!" he urged her; but she kept on repeating: "Why do you want to sit in front?"

"Because I—because I want to feel you holding me," he stammered, and dragged her to her feet.

The answer seemed to satisfy her, or else she yielded to the power of his voice. He bent down, feeling in the obscurity for the glassy slide worn by preceding coasters, and placed the runners carefully between its edges. She waited while he seated himself with crossed legs in the front of the sled; then she crouched quickly down at his back and clasped her arms about him. Her breath in his neck set him shuddering again, and he almost sprang from his seat. But in a flash he remembered the alternative. She was right: this was better than parting. He leaned back and drew her mouth to his. . .

Just as they started he heard the sorrel's whinny again, and the familiar wistful call, and all the confused images it brought with it, went with him down the first reach of the road. Half-way down there was a sudden drop, then a rise, and after that another long delirious descent. As they took wing for this it seemed to him that they were flying indeed, flying far up into the cloudy night, with Starkfield immeasurably below them, falling away like a speck in space. . . Then the big elm shot up ahead, lying in wait for them at the bend of the road, and he said between his teeth: "We can fetch it; I know we can fetch it—"

As they flew toward the tree Mattie pressed her arms tighter, and her blood seemed to be in his veins. Once or twice the sled swerved a little under them. He slanted his body to keep it headed for the elm, repeating to himself again and again: "I know we can fetch it"; and little phrases she had spoken ran through his head and danced before him on the air. The big tree loomed bigger and closer, and as they bore down on it he thought: "It's waiting for us: it seems to know." But suddenly his wife's face, with twisted monstrous lineaments, thrust itself between him and his goal, and he made an instinctive movement to brush it aside. The sled swerved in response, but he righted it again, kept it straight, and drove down on the black projecting mass. There was a last instant when the air shot past him like millions of fiery wires; and then the elm . . .

The sky was still thick, but looking straight up he saw a single star, and tried vaguely to reckon whether it were Sirius, or—or— The effort tired him too much, and he closed his heavy lids and thought that he would sleep. . . The stillness was so profound that he heard a little animal twittering somewhere near by under the snow. It made a small frightened *cheep* like a field mouse, and he wondered languidly if it were hurt. Then he understood that it must be in pain: pain so excruciating that he seemed, mysteriously, to feel it shooting through his own body. He tried in vain to roll over in the direction of the sound, and stretched his left arm out across the snow. And now it was as though he felt rather than heard the twittering; it seemed to be under his palm, which rested on something soft and springy. The thought of the animal's suffering was intolerable to him and he struggled to raise himself, and could not because a rock, or some huge mass, seemed to be lying on him. But he continued to finger about cautiously with his left hand, thinking he might get hold of the little creature and help it; and all at once he knew that the soft thing he had touched was Mattie's hair and that his hand was on her face.

He dragged himself to his knees, the monstrous load on him moving with him as he moved, and his hand went over and over her face, and he felt that the twittering came from her lips . . .

He got his face down close to hers, with his ear to her mouth, and in the darkness he saw her eyes open and heard her say his name.

"Oh, Matt, I thought we'd fetched it," he moaned; and far off, up the hill, he heard the sorrel whinny, and thought: "I ought to be getting him his feed. . ."

The querulous drone ceased as I entered Frome's kitchen, and of the two women sitting there I could not tell which had been the speaker.

One of them, on my appearing, raised her tall bony figure from her seat, not as if to welcome me—for she threw me no more than a brief glance of surprise—but simply to set about preparing the meal which Frome's absence had delayed. A slatternly calico wrapper hung from her shoulders and the wisps of her thin gray hair were drawn away from a high forehead and fastened at the back by a broken comb. She had pale opaque eyes which revealed nothing and reflected nothing, and her narrow lips were of the same sallow colour as her face.

The other woman was much smaller and slighter. She sat huddled in an arm-chair near the stove, and when I came in she turned her head quickly toward me, without the least corresponding movement of her body. Her hair was as gray as her companion's.

Great was her amazement, and that of old Mrs. Varnum, on learning that Ethan Frome's old horse had carried me to and from Corbury Junction through the worst blizzard of the winter; greater still their surprise when they heard that his master had taken me in for the night.

Beneath their wondering exclamations I felt a secret curiosity to know what impressions I had received from my night in the Frome household, and divined that the best way of breaking down their reserve was to let them try to penetrate mine. I therefore confined myself to saying, in a matter-of-fact tone, that I had been received with great kindness, and that Frome had made a bed for me in a room on the ground-floor which seemed in happier days to have been fitted up as a kind of writing-room or study.

"Well," Mrs. Hale mused, "in such a storm I suppose he felt he couldn't do less than take you in—but I guess it went hard with Ethan. I don't believe but what you're the only stranger has set foot in that house for over twenty years. He's that proud he don't even like his oldest friends to go there; and I don't know as any do, any more, except myself and the doctor. . ."

"You still go there, Mrs. Hale?" I ventured.

"I used to go a good deal after the accident, when I was first married; but after awhile I got to think it made 'em feel worse to see us. And then one thing and another came, and my own troubles . . . But I generally make out to drive over there round about New Year's, and once in the summer. Only I always try to pick a day when Ethan's off somewheres. It's bad enough to see the two women sitting there—but *his* face, when he looks round that bare place, just kills me . . . You see, I can look back and call it up in his mother's day, before their troubles."

Old Mrs. Varnum, by this time, had gone up to bed, and her daughter and I were sitting alone, after supper, in the austere seclusion of the horse-hair parlour. Mrs. Hale glanced at me tentatively, as though trying to see how much footing my conjectures gave her; and I guessed that if she had kept silence till now it was because she had been waiting, through all the years, for some one who should see what she alone had seen.

I waited to let her trust in me gather strength before I said: "Yes, it's pretty bad, seeing all three of them there together."

She drew her mild brows into a frown of pain. "It was just awful from the beginning. I was here in the house when they were carried up—they laid Mattie Silver in the room you're in. She and I were great friends, and she was to have been my bridesmaid in the spring . . . When she came to I went up to her and stayed all night. They gave her things to quiet her, and she didn't know much till to'rd morning, and then all of a sudden she woke up just like herself, and looked straight at me out of her big eyes, and said . . . Oh, I don't know why I'm telling you all this," Mrs. Hale broke off, crying.

She took off her spectacles, wiped the moisture from them, and put them on again with an unsteady hand. "It got about the next day," she went on, "that Zeena Frome had sent Mattie off in a hurry because she had a hired girl coming, and the folks here could never rightly tell what she and Ethan were doing that night coasting, when they'd ought to have been on their way to the

Flats to ketch the train . . . I never knew myself what Zeena thought—I don't to this day. Nobody knows Zeena's thoughts. Anyhow, when she heard o' the accident she came right in and stayed with Ethan over to the minister's, where they'd carried him. And as soon as the doctors said that Mattie could be moved, Zeena sent for her and took her back to the farm."

"And there she's been ever since?"

Mrs. Hale answered simply: "There was nowhere else for her to go;" and my heart tightened at the thought of the hard compulsions of the poor.

"Yes, there she's been," Mrs. Hale continued, "and Zeena's done for her, and done for Ethan, as good as she could. It was a miracle, considering how sick she was—but she seemed to be raised right up just when the call came to her. Not as she's ever given up doctoring, and she's had sick spells right along; but she's had the strength given her to care for those two for over twenty years, and before the accident came she thought she couldn't even care for herself."

Mrs. Hale paused a moment, and I remained silent, plunged in the vision of what her words evoked. "It's horrible for them all," I murmured.

"Yes: it's pretty bad. And they ain't any of 'em easy people either. Mattie *was*, before the accident; I never knew a sweeter nature. But she's suffered too much—that's what I always say when folks tell me how she's soured. And Zeena, she was always cranky. Not but what she bears with Mattie wonderful—I've seen that myself. But sometimes the two of them get going at each other, and then Ethan's face'd break your heart . . . When I see that, I think it's *him* that suffers most . . . anyhow it ain't Zeena, because she ain't got the time . . . It's a pity, though," Mrs. Hale ended, sighing, "that they're all shut up there'n that one kitchen. In the summertime, on pleasant days, they move Mattie into the parlour, or out in the door-yard, and that makes it easier . . . but winters there's the fires to be thought of; and there ain't a dime to spare up at the Fromes.'"

Mrs. Hale drew a deep breath, as though her memory were eased of its long burden, and she had no more to say: but suddenly an impulse of complete avowal seized her.

She took off her spectacles again, leaned toward me across the bead-word table-cover, and went on with lowered voice: "There was one day, about a week after the accident, when they all thought Mattie couldn't live. Well, I say it's a pity she *did*. I said it right out to our minister once, and he was shocked at me. Only he wasn't with me that morning when she first came to . . . And I say, if she'd ha' died, Ethan might ha' lived; and the way they are now, I don't see's there's much difference between the Fromes up at the farm and the Fromes down in the graveyard; 'cept that down there they're all quiet, and the women have got to hold their tongues."

. . .

THE OTHER TWO

CHAPTER 1

Waythorn, on the drawing-room hearth, waited for his wife to come down to dinner.

It was their first night under his own roof, and he was surprised at his thrill of boyish agitation. He was not so old, to be sure—his glass gave him little more than the five-and-thirty years to which his wife confessed—but he had fancied himself already in the temperate zone; yet here he was listening for her step with a tender sense of all it symbolised, with some old trail of verse about the garlanded nuptial door-posts floating through his enjoyment of the pleasant room and the good dinner just beyond it.

They had been hastily recalled from their honeymoon by the illness of Lily Haskett, the child of Mrs. Waythorn's first marriage. The little girl, at Waythorn's desire, had been transferred to his house on the day of her mother's wedding, and the doctor, on their arrival, broke the news that she was ill with typhoid, but declared that all the symptoms were favourable. Lily could show twelve years of unblemished health, and the case promised to be a light one. The nurse spoke as reassuringly, and after a moment of alarm Mrs. Waythorn had adjusted herself to the situation. She was very fond of Lily—her affection for the child had perhaps been her decisive charm in Waythorn's eyes—but she had the perfectly balanced nerves which her little girl had inherited, and no woman ever wasted less tissue in unproductive worry. Waythorn was therefore quite prepared to see her come in presently, a little late because of a last look at Lily, but as serene and well-appointed as if her good-night kiss had been laid on the brow of health. Her composure was restful to him; it acted as ballast to his somewhat unstable sensibilities. As he pictured her bending over the child's bed he thought how soothing her presence must be in illness: her very step would prognosticate recovery.

His own life had been a gray one, from temperament rather than circumstance, and he had been drawn to her by the unperturbed gaiety which kept her fresh and elastic at an age when most women's activities are growing either slack or febrile. He knew what was said about her; for, popular as she was, there had always been a faint undercurrent of detraction. When she had appeared in New York, nine or ten years earlier, as the pretty Mrs. Haskett whom Gus Varick had unearthed somewhere—was it in Pittsburg or Utica?—society, while promptly accepting her, had reserved the right to cast a doubt on its own indiscrimination. Enquiry, however, established her undoubted connection with a socially reigning family, and explained her recent divorce as the natural result of a runaway match at seventeen; and as nothing was known of Mr. Haskett it was easy to believe the worst of him.

Alice Haskett's remarriage with Gus Varick was a passport to the set whose recognition she coveted, and for a few years the Varicks were the most popular couple in town. Unfortunately the alliance was brief and stormy, and this time the husband had his champions. Still, even Varick's stanchest supporters admitted that he was not meant for matrimony, and Mrs. Varick's grievances were of a nature to bear the inspection of the New York courts. A New York divorce is in itself a diploma of virtue, and in the semi-widowhood of this second separation Mrs. Varick took on an air of sanctity, and was allowed to confide her wrongs to some of the most scrupulous ears in town. But when it was known that she was to marry Waythorn there was a momentary reaction. Her best friends would have preferred to see her remain in the rôle of the injured wife, which was as becoming to her as crape to a rosy complexion. True, a decent time had elapsed, and it was not even suggested that Waythorn had supplanted his predecessor. People shook their heads over him, however, and one grudging friend, to whom he affirmed that he took the step with his eyes open, replied oracularly: "Yes—and with your ears shut."

Waythorn could afford to smile at these innuendoes. In the Wall Street phrase, he had "discounted" them. He knew that society has not yet adapted itself to the consequences of divorce, and that till the adaptation takes place every woman who uses the freedom the law accords her must be her own social justification.

Waythorn had an amused confidence in his wife's ability to justify herself. His expectations were fulfilled, and before the wedding took place Alice Varick's group had rallied openly to her support. She took it all imperturbably: she had a way of surmounting obstacles without seeming to be aware of them, and Waythorn looked back with wonder at the trivialities over which he had worn his nerves thin. He had the sense of having found refuge in a richer, warmer nature than his own, and his satisfaction, at the moment, was humourously summed up in the thought that his wife, when she had done all she could for Lily, would not be ashamed to come down and enjoy a good dinner.

The anticipation of such enjoyment was not, however, the sentiment expressed by Mrs. Waythorn's charming face when she presently joined him. Though she had put on her most engaging tea-gown she had neglected to assume the smile that went with it, and Waythorn thought he had never seen her look so nearly worried.

"What is it?" he asked. "Is anything wrong with Lily?"

"No; I've just been in and she's still sleeping." Mrs. Waythorn hesitated. "But something tiresome has happened."

He had taken her two hands, and now perceived that he was crushing a paper between them.

"This letter?"

"Yes—Mr. Haskett has written—I mean his lawyer has written."

Waythorn felt himself flush uncomfortably. He dropped his wife's hands.

"What about?"

"About seeing Lily. You know the courts—"

"Yes, yes," he interrupted nervously.

Nothing was known about Haskett in New York. He was vaguely supposed to have remained in the outer darkness from which his wife had been rescued, and Waythorn was one of the few who were aware that he had given up his business in Utica and followed her to New York in order to be near his little girl. In the days of his wooing, Waythorn had often met Lily on the doorstep, rosy and smiling, on her way "to see papa."

"I am so sorry," Mrs. Waythorn murmured.

He roused himself. "What does he want?"

"He wants to see her. You know she goes to him once a week."

"Well—he doesn't expect her to go to him now, does he?"

"No—he has heard of her illness; but he expects to come here."

"*Here?*"

Mrs. Waythorn reddened under his gaze. They looked away from each other.

"I'm afraid he has the right. . . . You'll see. . . ." She made a proffer of the letter.

Waythorn moved away with a gesture of refusal. He stood staring about the softly lighted room, which a moment before had seemed so full of bridal intimacy.

"I'm so sorry," she repeated. "If Lily could have been moved—"

"That's out of the question," he returned impatiently.

"I suppose so."

Her lip was beginning to tremble, and he felt himself a brute.

"He must come, of course," he said. "When is—his day?"

"I'm afraid—to-morrow."

"Very well. Send a note in the morning."

The butler entered to announce dinner.

Waythorn turned to his wife. "Come—you must be tired. It's beastly, but try to forget about it," he said, drawing her hand through his arm.

"You're so good, dear. I'll try," she whispered back.

Her face cleared at once, and as she looked at him across the flowers, between the rosy candle-shades, he saw her lips waver back into a smile.

"How pretty everything is!" she sighed luxuriously.

He turned to the butler. "The champagne at once, please. Mrs. Waythorn is tired."

In a moment or two their eyes met above the sparkling glasses. Her own were quite clear and untroubled: he saw that she had obeyed his injunction and forgotten.

CHAPTER 2

Waythorn, the next morning, went down town earlier than usual. Haskett was not likely to come till the afternoon, but the instinct of flight drove him forth. He meant to stay away all day—he had thoughts of dining at his club. As his door closed behind him he reflected that before he opened it again it would have admitted another man who had as much right to enter it as himself, and the thought filled him with a physical repugnance.

He caught the "elevated" at the employés' hour, and found himself crushed between two layers of pendulous humanity. At Eighth Street the man facing him wriggled out, and another took his place. Waythorn glanced up and saw that it was Gus Varick. The men were so close together that it was impossible to ignore the smile of recognition on Varick's handsome overblown face. And after all—why not? They had always been on good terms, and Varick had been divorced before Waythorn's attentions to his wife began. The two exchanged a word on the perennial grievance of the congested trains, and when a seat at their side was miraculously left empty the instinct of self-preservation made Waythorn slip into it after Varick.

The latter drew the stout man's breath of relief. "Lord—I was beginning to feel like a pressed flower." He leaned back, looking unconcernedly at Waythorn. "Sorry to hear that Sellers is knocked out again."

"Sellers?" echoed Waythorn, starting at his partner's name.

Varick looked surprised. "You didn't know he was laid up with the gout?"

"No. I've been away—I only got back last night." Waythorn felt himself reddening in anticipation of the other's smile.

"Ah—yes; to be sure. And Seller's attack came on two days ago. I'm afraid he's pretty bad. Very awkward for me, as it happens, because he was just putting through a rather important thing for me."

"Ah?" Waythorn wondered vaguely since when Varick had

been dealing in "important things." Hitherto he had dabbled only in the shallow pools of speculation, with which Waythorn's office did not usually concern itself.

It occurred to him that Varick might be talking at random, to relieve the strain of their propinquity. That strain was becoming momentarily more apparent to Waythorn, and when, at Cortlandt Street, he caught sight of an acquaintance and had a sudden vision of the picture he and Varick must present to an initiated eye, he jumped up with a muttered excuse.

"I hope you'll find Sellers better," said Varick civilly, and he stammered back: "If I can be of any use to you—" and let the departing crowd sweep him to the platform.

At his office he heard that Sellers was in fact ill with the gout, and would probably not be able to leave the house for some weeks.

"I'm sorry it should have happened so, Mr. Waythorn," the senior clerk said with affable significance. "Mr. Sellers was very much upset at the idea of giving you such a lot of extra work just now."

"Oh, that's no matter," said Waythorn hastily. He secretly welcomed the pressure of additional business, and was glad to think that, when the day's work was over, he would have to call at his partner's on the way home.

He was late for luncheon, and turned in at the nearest restaurant instead of going to his club. The place was full, and the waiter hurried him to the back of the room to capture the only vacant table. In the cloud of cigar-smoke Waythorn did not at once distinguish his neighbours: but presently, looking about him, he saw Varick seated a few feet off. This time, luckily, they were too far apart for conversation, and Varick, who faced another way, had probably not even seen him; but there was an irony in their renewed nearness.

Varick was said to be fond of good living, and as Waythorn sat despatching his hurried luncheon he looked across half enviously at the other's leisurely degustation of his meal. When Waythorn first saw him he had been helping himself with critical deliberation to a bit of Camembert at the ideal point of liquefaction, and now, the cheese removed, he was just pouring his *café double* from its little two-storied earthen pot. He poured slowly, his ruddy profile bent above the task, and one beringed white hand steadying the lid of the coffee-pot; then he stretched his other hand to the decanter of cognac at his elbow, filled a liqueur-glass, took a tentative sip, and poured the brandy into his coffee-cup.

Waythorn watched him in a kind of fascination. What was he thinking of—only of the flavour of the coffee and the liqueur? Had the morning's meeting left no more trace in his thoughts than on his face? Had his wife so completely passed out of his life that even this odd encounter with her present husband, within a week after her remarriage, was no more than an incident in his day? And as Waythorn mused, another idea struck him: had Haskett ever met Varick as Varick and he had just met? The recollection of Haskett perturbed him, and he rose and left the restaurant, taking a circuitous way out to escape the placid irony of Varick's nod.

It was after seven when Waythorn reached home. He thought the footman who opened the door looked at him oddly.

"How is Miss Lily?" he asked in haste.

"Doing very well, sir. A gentleman—."

"Tell Barlow to put off dinner for half an hour," Waythorn cut him off, hurrying upstairs.

He went straight to his room and dressed without seeing his wife. When he reached the drawing-room she was there, fresh and radiant. Lily's day had been good; the doctor was not coming back that evening.

At dinner Waythorn told her of Sellers's illness and of the resulting complications. She listened sympathetically, adjuring him not to let himself be overworked, and asking vague feminine questions about the routine of the office. Then she gave him the chronicle of Lily's day; quoted the nurse and doctor, and told him who had called to inquire. He had never seen her more serene and unruffled. It struck him, with a curious pang, that she was very happy in being with him, so happy that she found a childish pleasure in rehearsing the trivial incidents of her day.

After dinner they went to the library, and the servant put the coffee and liqueurs on a low table before her and left the room. She looked singularly soft and girlish in her rosy pale dress, against the dark leather of one of his bachelor armchairs. A day earlier the contrast would have charmed him.

He turned away now, choosing a cigar with affected delibera-tion.

"Did Haskett come?" he asked, with his back to her.

"Oh, yes—he came."

"You didn't see him, of course?"

She hesitated a moment. "I let the nurse see him."

That was all. There was nothing more to ask. He swung round toward her, applying a match to his cigar. Well, the thing was over for a week, at any rate. He would try not to think of it. She looked up at him, a trifle rosier than usual, with a smile in her eyes.

"Ready for your coffee, dear?"

He leaned against the mantelpiece, watching her as she lifted the coffee-pot. The lamplight struck a gleam from her bracelets and tipped her soft hair with brightness. How light and slender she was, and how each gesture flowed into the next! She seemed a creature all compact of harmonies. As the thought of Haskett receded, Waythorn felt himself yielding again to the joy of posses-sorship. They were his, those white hands with their flitting motions, his the light haze of hair, the lips and eyes. . . .

She set down the coffee-pot, and reaching for the decanter of cognac, measured off a liqueur-glass and poured it into his cup.

Waythorn uttered a sudden exclamation.

"What is the matter?" she said, startled.

"Nothing; only—I don't take cognac in my coffee."

"Oh, how stupid of me," she cried.

Their eyes met, and she blushed a sudden agonised red.

CHAPTER 3

Ten days later, Mr. Sellers, still house-bound, asked Waythorn to call on his way down town.

The senior partner, with his swaddled foot propped up by the fire, greeted his associate with an air of embarrassment.

"I'm sorry, my dear fellow; I've got to ask you to do an awkward thing for me."

Waythorn waited, and the other went on, after a pause apparently given to the arrangement of his phrases: "The fact is, when I was knocked out I had just gone into a rather complicated piece of business for—Gus Varick."

"Well?" said Waythorn, with an attempt to put him at his ease.

"Well—it's this way: Varick came to me the day before my attack. He had evidently had an inside tip from somebody, and had made about a hundred thousand. He came to me for advice, and I suggested his going in with Vanderlyn."

"Oh, the deuce!" Waythorn exclaimed. He saw in a flash what had happened. The investment was an alluring one, but required negotiation. He listened quietly while Sellers put the case before him, and, the statement ended, he said: "You think I ought to see Varick?"

"I'm afraid I can't as yet. The doctor is obdurate. And this thing can't wait. I hate to ask you, but no one else in the office knows the ins and outs of it."

Waythorn stood silent. He did not care a farthing for the success of Varick's venture, but the honour of the office was to be considered, and he could hardly refuse to oblige his partner.

"Very well," he said, "I'll do it."

That afternoon, apprised by telephone, Varick called at the office. Waythorn, waiting in his private room, wondered what the others thought of it. The newspapers, at the time of Mrs. Waythorn's marriage, had acquainted their readers with every detail of her previous matrimonial ventures, and Waythorn could fancy the clerks smiling behind Varick's back as he was ushered in.

Varick bore himself admirably. He was easy without being undignified, and Waythorn was conscious of cutting a much less impressive figure. Varick had no experience of business, and the talk prolonged itself for nearly an hour while Waythorn set forth with scrupulous precision the details of the proposed transaction.

"I'm awfully obliged to you," Varick said as he rose. "The fact is I'm not used to having much money to look after, and I don't want to make an ass of myself—" He smiled, and Waythorn could not help noticing that there was something pleasant about his smile. "If feels uncommonly queer to have enough cash to pay one's bills. I'd have sold my soul for it a few years ago!"

Waythorn winced at the allusion. He had heard it rumoured that a lack of funds had been one of the determining causes of the Varick separation, but it did not occur to him that Varick's words were intentional. It seemed more likely that the desire to keep clear of embarrassing topics had fatally drawn him into one. Waythorn did not wish to be outdone in civility.

"We'll do the best we can for you," he said. "I think this is a good thing you're in."

"Oh, I'm sure it's immense. It's awfully good of you—" Varick broke off, embarrassed. "I suppose the thing's settled now—but if—"

"If anything happens before Sellers is about, I'll see you again," said Waythorn quietly. He was glad, in the end, to appear the more self-possessed of the two.

•   •   •

The course of Lily's illness ran smooth, and as the days passed Waythorn grew used to the idea of Haskett's weekly visit. The first time the day came round, he stayed out late, and questioned his wife as to the visit on his return. She replied at once that Haskett had merely seen the nurse downstairs, as the doctor did not wish any one in the child's sick-room till after the crisis.

The following week Waythorn was again conscious of the recurrence of the day, but had forgotten it by the time he came home to dinner. The crisis of the disease came a few days later, with a rapid decline of fever, and the little girl was pronounced out of danger. In the rejoicing which ensued the thought of Haskett passed out of Waythorn's mind, and one afternoon, letting himself into the house with a latchkey, he went straight to his library without noticing a shabby hat and umbrella in the hall.

In the library he found a small effaced-looking man with a thinnish gray beard sitting on the edge of a chair. The stranger might have been a piano-tuner, or one of those mysteriously efficient persons who are summoned in emergencies to adjust some detail of the domestic machinery. He blinked at Waythorn through a pair of gold-rimmed spectacles and said mildly: "Mr. Waythorn, I presume? I am Lily's father."

Waythorn flushed. "Oh—" he stammered uncomfortably. He broke off, disliking to appear rude. Inwardly he was trying to adjust the actual Haskett to the image of him projected by his wife's reminiscences. Waythorn had been allowed to infer that Alice's first husband was a brute.

"I am sorry to intrude," said Haskett, with his over-the-counter politeness.

"Don't mention it," returned Waythorn, collecting himself. "I suppose the nurse has been told?"

"I presume so. I can wait," said Haskett. He had a resigned way of speaking, as though life had worn down his natural powers of resistance.

Waythorn stood on the threshold, nervously pulling off his gloves.

"I'm sorry you've been detained. I will send for the nurse," he said; and as he opened the door he added with an effort: "I'm glad we can give you a good report of Lily." He winced as the *we* slipped out, but Haskett seemed not to notice it.

"Thank you, Mr. Waythorn. It's been an anxious time for me."

"Ah, well, that's past. Soon she'll be able to go to you." Waythorn nodded and passed out.

In his own room he flung himself down with a groan. He hated the womanish sensibility which made him suffer so acutely from the grotesque chances of life. He had known when he married that his wife's former husbands were both living, and that amid the multiplied contacts of modern existence there were a thousand chances to one that he would run against one or the other, yet he found himself as much disturbed by his brief encounter with Haskett as though the law had not obligingly removed all difficulties in the way of their meeting.

Waythorn sprang up and began to pace the room nervously. He had not suffered half as much from his two meetings with Varick. It was Haskett's presence in his own house that made the situation so intolerable. He stood still, hearing steps in the passage.

"This way, please," he heard the nurse say. Haskett was being taken upstairs, then: not a corner of the house but was open to him. Waythorn dropped into another chair, staring vaguely ahead of him. On his dressing-table stood a photograph of Alice, taken when he had first known her. She was Alice Varick then—how fine and exquisite he had thought her! Those were Varick's pearls about her neck. At Waythorn's instance they had been returned before her marriage. Had Haskett ever given her any trinkets— and what had become of them, Waythorn wondered? He realised suddenly that he knew very little of Haskett's past or present situation; but from the man's appearance and manner of speech he could reconstruct with curious precision the surroundings of Alice's first marriage. And it startled him to think that she had, in the background of her life, a phase of existence so different from anything with which he had connected her. Varick, whatever his faults, was a gentleman, in the conventional, traditional sense of the term: the sense which at that moment seemed, oddly enough, to have most meaning to Waythorn. He and Varick had the same social habits, spoke the same language, understood the same allusions. But this other man . . . it was grotesquely uppermost in Waythorn's mind that Haskett had worn a made-up tie attached with an elastic. Why should that ridiculous detail symbolise the whole man? Waythorn was exasperated by his own paltriness, but the fact of the tie expanded, forced itself on him, became as it were the key to Alice's past. He could see her, as Mrs. Haskett, sitting in a "front parlour" furnished in plush, with a pianola, and a copy of "Ben Hur" on the centre-table. He could see her going to the theatre with Haskett—or perhaps even to a "Church Sociable"—she in a "picture hat" and Haskett in a black frock-coat, a little creased, with the made-up tie on an elastic. On the way home they would stop and look at the illuminated shop-windows, lingering over the photographs of New York actresses. On Sunday afternoons Haskett would take her for a walk, pushing Lily ahead of them in a white enamelled perambulator, and Waythorn had a vision of the people they would stop and talk to. He could fancy how pretty Alice must have looked, in a dress adroitly constructed from the hints of a New York fashion-paper, and how she must have looked down on the other women, chafing at her life, and secretly feeling that she belonged in a bigger place.

For the moment his foremost thought was one of wonder at the way in which she had shed the phase of existence which her marriage with Haskett implied. It was as if her whole aspect, every gesture, every inflection, every allusion, were a studied negation of that period in her life. If she had denied being married to Haskett she could hardly have stood more convicted of duplicity than in this obliteration of the self which had been his wife.

Waythorn started up, checking himself in the analysis of her motives. What right had he to create a fantastic effigy of her and then pass judgment on it? She had spoken vaguely of her first marriage as unhappy, had hinted, with becoming reticence, that Haskett had wrought havoc among her young illusions. . . . It was a pity for Waythorn's peace of mind that Haskett's very inoffensiveness shed a new light on the nature of those illusions. A man would rather think that his wife has been brutalised by her first husband than that the process has been reversed.

CHAPTER 4

"Mr. Waythorn, I don't like that French governess of Lily's."

Haskett, subdued and apologetic, stood before Waythorn in the library, revolving his shabby hat in his hand.

Waythorn, surprised in his armchair over the evening paper, stared back perplexedly at his visitor.

"You'll excuse my asking to see you," Haskett continued. "But this is my last visit, and I thought if I could have a word with you it would be a better way than writing to Mrs. Waythorn's lawyer."

Waythorn rose uneasily. He did not like the French governess either; but that was irrelevant.

"I am not so sure of that," he returned stiffly; "but since you wish it I will give your message to—my wife." He always hesitated over the possessive pronoun in addressing Haskett.

The latter sighed. "I don't know as that will help much. She didn't like it when I spoke to her."

Waythorn turned red. "When did you see her?" he asked.

"Not since the first day I came to see Lily—right after she was taken sick. I remarked to her then that I didn't like the governess."

Waythorn made no answer. He remembered distinctly that, after that first visit, he had asked his wife if she had seen Haskett. She had lied to him then, but she had respected his wishes since; and the incident cast a curious light on her character. He was sure she would not have seen Haskett that first day if she had divined that Waythorn would object, and the fact that she did not divine it was almost as disagreeable to the latter as the discovery that she had lied to him.

"I don't like the woman," Haskett was repeating with mild persistency. "She ain't straight, Mr. Waythorn—she'll teach the child to be underhand. I've noticed a change in Lily—she's too anxious to please—and she don't always tell the truth. She used to be the straightest child, Mr. Waythorn—" He broke off, his voice a little thick. "Not but what I want her to have a stylish education," he ended.

Waythorn was touched. "I'm sorry, Mr. Haskett; but frankly, I don't quite see what I can do."

Haskett hesitated. Then he laid his hat on the table, and advanced to the hearth-rug, on which Waythorn was standing. There was nothing aggressive in his manner, but he had the solemnity of a timid man resolved on a decisive measure.

"There's just one thing you can do, Mr. Waythorn," he said. "You can remind Mrs. Waythorn that, by the decree of the courts, I am entitled to have a voice in Lily's bringing up." He paused, and went on more deprecatingly: "I'm not the kind to talk about enforcing my rights, Mr. Waythorn. I don't know as I think a man is entitled to rights he hasn't known how to hold on to; but this business of the child is different. I've never let go there—and I never mean to."

• • •

The scene left Waythorn deeply shaken. Shamefacedly, in indirect ways, he had been finding out about Haskett; and all that he had learned was favourable. The little man, in order to be near his daughter, had sold out his share in a profitable business in Utica, and accepted a modest clerkship in a New York manufacturing house. He boarded in a shabby street and had few acquaintances. His passion for Lily filled his life. Waythorn felt that this exploration of Haskett was like groping about with a dark-lantern in his wife's past; but he saw now that there were recesses his lantern had not explored. He had never enquired into the exact circumstances of his wife's first matrimonial rupture. On the surface all had been fair. It was she who had obtained the divorce, and the court had given her the child. But Waythorn knew how many ambiguities such a verdict might cover. The mere fact that Haskett retained a right over his daughter implied an unsuspected compromise. Waythorn was an idealist. He always refused to recognise unpleasant contingencies till he found himself confronted with them, and then he saw them followed by a spectral train of consequences. His next days were thus haunted, and he determined to try to lay the ghosts by conjuring them up in his wife's presence.

When he repeated Haskett's request a flame of anger passed over her face; but she subdued it instantly and spoke with a slight quiver of outraged motherhood.

"It is very ungentlemanly of him," she said.

The word grated on Waythorn. "That is neither here nor there. It's a bare question of rights."

She murmured: "It's not as if he could ever be a help to Lily—"

Waythorn flushed. This was even less to his taste. "The question is," he repeated, "what authority has he over her?"

She looked downward, twisting herself a little in her seat. "I am willing to see him—I thought you objected," she faltered.

In a flash he understood that she knew the extent of Haskett's claims. Perhaps it was not the first time she had resisted them.

"My objecting has nothing to do with it," he said coldly; "if Haskett has a right to be consulted you must consult him."

She burst into tears, and he saw that she expected him to regard her as a victim.

Haskett did not abuse his rights. Waythorn had felt miserably sure that he would not. But the governess was dismissed, and from time to time the little man demanded an interview with Alice. After the first outburst she accepted the situation with her usual adaptability. Haskett had once reminded Waythorn of the piano-tuner, and Mrs. Waythorn, after a month or two, appeared to class him with that domestic familiar. Waythorn could not but respect the father's tenacity. At first he had tried to cultivate the suspicion that Haskett might be "up to" something, that he had an object in securing a foothold in the house. But in his heart Waythorn was sure of Haskett's single-mindedness; he even guessed in the latter a mild contempt for such advantages as his relation with the Waythorns might offer. Haskett's sincerity of purpose made him invulnerable, and his successor had to accept him as a lien on the property.

•　•　•

Mr. Sellers was sent to Europe to recover from his gout, and Varick's affairs hung on Waythorn's hands. The negotiations were prolonged and complicated; they necessitated frequent conferences between the two men, and the interests of the firm forbade Waythorn's suggesting that his client should transfer his business to another office.

Varick appeared well in the transaction. In moments of relaxation his coarse streak appeared, and Waythorn dreaded his geniality; but in the office he was concise and clear-headed, with a flattering deference to Waythorn's judgment. Their business relations being so affably established, it would have been absurd for the two men to ignore each other in society. The first time they met in a drawing-room, Varick took up their intercourse in the same easy key, and his hostess's grateful glance obliged Waythorn to respond to it. After that they ran across each other frequently, and one evening at a ball Waythorn, wandering through the remoter rooms, came upon Varick seated beside his wife. She coloured a little, and faltered in what she was saying; but Varick nodded to Waythorn without rising, and the latter strolled on.

In the carriage, on the way home, he broke out nervously: "I didn't know you spoke to Varick."

Her voice trembled a little. "It's the first time—he happened to be standing near me; I didn't know what to do. It's so awkward, meeting everywhere—and he said you had been very kind about some business."

"That's different," said Waythorn.

She paused a moment. "I'll do just as you wish," she returned pliantly. "I thought it would be less awkward to speak to him when we meet."

Her pliancy was beginning to sicken him. Had she really no will of her own—no theory about her relation to these men? She had accepted Haskett—did she mean to accept Varick? It was "less awkward," as she had said, and her instinct was to evade difficulties or to circumvent them. With sudden vividness Waythorn saw how the instinct had developed. She was "as easy as an old shoe"— a shoe that too many feet had worn. Her elasticity was the result of tension in too many different directions. Alice Haskett—Alice Varick—Alice Waythorn—she had been each in turn, and had left hanging to each name a little of her privacy, a little of her personality, a little of the inmost self where the unknown god abides.

"Yes—it's better to speak to Varick," said Waythorn wearily.

CHAPTER 5

The winter wore on, and society took advantage of the Waythorns' acceptance of Varick. Harassed hostesses were grateful to them for bridging over a social difficulty, and Mrs. Waythorn was help up as a miracle of good taste. Some experimental spirits could not resist the diversion of throwing Varick and his former wife together, and there were those who thought he found a zest in the propinquity. But Mrs. Waythorn's conduct remained irreproachable. She neither avoided Varick nor sought him out. Even Waythorn could not but admit that she had discovered the solution of the newest social problem.

He had married her without giving much thought to that problem. He had fancied that a woman can shed her past like a man. But now he saw that Alice was bound to hers both by the circumstances which forced her into continued relation with it, and by the traces it had left on her nature. With grim irony Waythorn compared himself to a member of a syndicate. He held so many shares in his wife's personality and his predecessors were his partners in the business. If there had been any element of passion in the transaction he would have felt less deteriorated by it. The fact that Alice took her change of husbands like a change of weather reduced the situation to mediocrity. He could have forgiven her for blunders, for excesses; for resisting Haskett, for yielding to Varick; for anything but her acquiescence and her tact. She reminded him of a juggler tossing knives; but the knives were blunt and she knew they would never cut her.

And then, gradually, habit formed a protecting surface for his sensibilities. If he paid for each day's comfort with the small change of his illusions, he grew daily to value the comfort more and set less store upon the coin. He had drifted into a dulling propinquity with Haskett and Varick and he took refuge in the cheap revenge of satirising the situation. He even began to reckon up the advantages which accrued from it, to ask himself if it were not better to own a third of a wife who knew how to make a man happy than a whole one who had lacked opportunity to acquire the art. For it *was* an art, and made up, like all others, of concessions, eliminations and embellishments; of lights judiciously thrown and shadows skilfully softened. His wife knew exactly how to manage the lights, and he knew exactly to what training she owed her skill. He even tried to trace the source of his obligations, to discriminate between the influences which had combined to produce his domestic happiness: he perceived that Haskett's commonness had made Alice worship good breeding, while Varick's liberal construction of the marriage bond had taught her to value the conjugal virtues; so that he was directly indebted to his predecessors for the devotion which made his life easy if not inspiring.

From this phase he passed into that of complete acceptance. He ceased to satirise himself because time dulled the irony of the situation and the joke lost its humour with its sting. Even the sight of Haskett's hat on the hall table had ceased to touch the springs of epigram. The hat was often seen there now, for it had been decided that it was better for Lily's father to visit her than for the little girl to go to his boarding-house. Waythorn, having acquiesced in this arrangement, had been surprised to find how little difference it made. Haskett was never obtrusive, and the few visitors who met him on the stairs were unaware of his identity. Waythorn did not know how often he saw Alice, but with himself Haskett was seldom in contact.

One afternoon, however, he learned on entering that Lily's father was waiting to see him. In the library he found Haskett occupying a chair in his usual provisional way. Waythorn always felt grateful to him for not leaning back.

"I hope you'll excuse me, Mr. Waythorn," he said rising. "I

wanted to see Mrs. Waythorn about Lily, and your man asked me to wait here till she came in."

"Of course," said Waythorn, remembering that a sudden leak had that morning given over the drawing-room to the plumbers.

He opened his cigar-case and held it out to his visitor, and Haskett's acceptance seemed to mark a fresh stage in their intercourse. The spring evening was chilly, and Waythorn invited his guest to draw up his chair to the fire. He meant to find an excuse to leave Haskett in a moment; but he was tired and cold, and after all the little man no longer jarred on him.

The two were enclosed in the intimacy of their blended cigar-smoke when the door opened and Varick walked into the room. Waythorn rose abruptly. It was the first time that Varick had come to the house, and the surprise of seeing him, combined with the singular inopportuneness of his arrival, gave a new edge to Waythorn's blunted sensibilities. He stared at his visitor without speaking.

Varick seemed too preoccupied to notice his host's embarrassment.

"My dear fellow," he exclaimed in his most expansive tone, "I must apologise for tumbling in on you in this way, but I was too late to catch you down town, and so I thought—"

He stopped short, catching sight of Haskett, and his sanguine colour deepened to a flush which spread vividly under his scant blond hair. But in a moment he recovered himself and nodded slightly. Haskett returned the bow in silence, and Waythorn was still groping for speech when the footman came in carrying a tea-table.

The intrusion offered a welcome vent to Waythorn's nerves. "What the deuce are you bringing this here for?" he said sharply.

"I beg your pardon, sir, but the plumbers are still in the drawing-room, and Mrs. Waythorn said she would have tea in the library." The footman's perfectly respectful tone implied a reflection on Waythorn's reasonableness.

"Oh, very well," said the latter resignedly, and the footman proceeded to open the folding tea-table and set out its complicated appointments. While this interminable process continued the three men stood motionless, watching it with a fascinated stare, till Waythorn, to break the silence, said to Varick: "Won't you have a cigar?"

He held out the case he had just tendered to Haskett, and Varick helped himself with a smile. Waythorn looked about for a match, and finding none, proffered a light from his own cigar. Haskett, in the background, held his ground mildly, examining his cigar-tip now and then, and stepping forward at the right moment to knock its ashes into the fire.

The footman at last withdrew, and Varick immediately began: "If I could just say half a word to you about this business—"

"Certainly," stammered Waythorn; "in the dining-room—"

But as he placed his hand on the door it opened from without, and his wife appeared on the threshold.

She came in fresh and smiling, in her street dress and hat, shedding a fragrance from the boa which she loosened in advancing.

"Shall we have tea in here, dear?" she began; and then she caught sight of Varick. Her smile deepened, veiling a slight tremor of surprise.

"Why, how do you do?" she said with a distinct note of pleasure.

As she shook hands with Varick she saw Haskett standing behind him. Her smile faded for a moment, but she recalled it quickly, with a scarcely perceptible side-glance at Waythorn.

"How do you do, Mr. Haskett?" she said, and shook hands with him a shade less cordially.

The three men stood awkwardly before her, till Varick, always the most self-possessed, dashed into an explanatory phrase.

"We—I had to see Waythorn a moment on business," he stammered, brick-red from chin to nape.

Haskett stepped forward with his air of mild obstinacy. "I am sorry to intrude; but you appointed five o'clock—" he directed his resigned glance to the time-piece on the mantel.

She swept aside their embarrassment with a charming gesture of hospitality.

"I'm so sorry—I'm always late; but the afternoon was so lovely."
She stood drawing off her gloves, propitiatory and graceful, diffusing about her a sense of ease and familiarity in which the situation
lost its grotesqueness. "But before talking business," she added
brightly, "I'm sure every one wants a cup of tea."

She dropped into her low chair by the tea-table, and the two
visitors, as if drawn by her smile, advanced to receive the cups
she held out.

She glanced about for Waythorn, and he took the third cup
with a laugh.

. . .

THE DILETTANTE

It was on an impulse hardly needing the arguments he found himself advancing in its favour, that Thursdale, on his way to the club, turned as usual into Mrs. Vervain's street.

The "as usual" was his own qualification of the act; a convenient way of bridging the interval—in days and other sequences—that lay between this visit and the last. It was characteristic of him that he instinctively excluded his call two days earlier, with Ruth Gaynor, from the list of his visits to Mrs. Vervain: the special conditions attending it had made it no more like a visit to Mrs. Vervain than an engraved dinner invitation is like a personal letter. Yet it was to talk over his call with Miss Gaynor that he was now returning to the scene of that episode; and it was because Mrs. Vervain could be trusted to handle the talking over as skilfully as the interview itself that, at her corner, he had felt the dilettante's irresistible craving to take a last look at a work of art that was passing out of his possession.

On the whole, he knew no one better fitted to deal with the unexpected than Mrs. Vervain. She excelled in the rare art of taking things for granted, and Thursdale felt a pardonable pride in the thought that she owed her excellence to his training. Early in his career Thursdale had made the mistake, at the outset of his acquaintance with a lady, of telling her that he loved her and exacting the same avowal in return. The latter part of that episode had been like the long walk back from a picnic, when one has to carry all the crockery one has finished using: it was the last time Thursdale ever allowed himself to be encumbered with the débris of a feast. He thus incidentally learned that the privilege of loving her is one of the least favours that a charming woman can accord; and in seeking to avoid the pitfalls of sentiment he had developed a science of evasion in which the woman of the moment became a mere implement of the game. He owed a great deal of delicate enjoyment to the cultivation of this art. The perils from which it had been his refuge became naïvely harmless: was it possible that he who now took his easy way along the levels had once preferred to gasp on the raw heights of emotion? Youth is a high-coloured season; but he had the satisfaction of feeling that he had entered earlier than most into that chiaroscuro of sensation where every half-tone has its value.

As a promoter of this pleasure no one he had known was comparable to Mrs. Vervain. He had taught a good many women not to betray their feelings, but he had never before had such fine material to work in. She had been surprisingly crude when he first knew her; capable of making the most awkward inferences, of plunging through thin ice, of recklessly undressing her emotions; but she had acquired, under the discipline of his reticences and evasions, a skill almost equal to his own, and perhaps more remarkable in that it involved keeping time with any tune he played and reading at sight some uncommonly difficult passages.

It had taken Thursdale seven years to form this fine talent; but the result justified the effort. At the crucial moment she had been perfect: her way of greeting Miss Gaynor had made him regret that he had announced his engagement by letter. It was an evasion that confessed a difficulty; a deviation implying an obstacle, where, by common consent, it was agreed to see none; it betrayed, in short, a lack of confidence in the completeness of his method. It had been his pride never to put himself in a position which had to be quitted, as it were, by the back door; but here, as he perceived, the main portals would have opened for him of their own accord. All this, and much more, he read in the finished naturalness with which Mrs. Vervain had met Miss Gaynor. He had never seen a better piece of work: there was no overeagerness, no suspicious warmth, above all (and this gave her art the grace of a natural quality) there were none of those damnable implications whereby a woman, in welcoming her friend's betrothed, may keep him on pins and needles while she laps the lady in complacency. So masterly a performance, indeed, hardly needed the offset of Miss Gaynor's door-step words—"To be so kind to me, how she must have liked you!"—though he caught himself wishing it lay within the bounds of fitness to transmit them, as a final tribute, to the one woman he knew who was unfailingly certain to enjoy a good thing. It was perhaps the one drawback to his new situation that it might develop good things which it would be impossible to hand on to Margaret Vervain.

The fact that he had made the mistake of underrating his friend's powers, the consciousness that his writing must have betrayed his distrust of her efficiency, seemed an added reason for turning down her street instead of going on to the club. He would show her that he knew how to value her; he would ask her to achieve with him a feat infinitely rarer and more delicate than the one he had appeared to avoid. Incidentally, he would also dispose of the interval of time before dinner: ever since he had seen Miss Gaynor off, an hour earlier, on her return journey to Buffalo, he had been wondering how he should put in the rest of the afternoon. It was absurd, how he missed the girl. . . . Yes, that was it: the desire to talk about her was, after all, at the bottom of his impulse to call on Mrs. Vervain! It was absurd, if you like—but it was delightfully rejuvenating. He could recall the time when he had been afraid of being obvious: now he felt that this return to the primitive emotions might be as restorative as a holiday in the Canadian woods. And it was precisely by the girl's candour, her directness, her lack of complications, that he was taken. The sense that she might say something rash at any moment was positively exhilarating: if she had thrown her arms about him at the station he would not have given a thought to his crumpled dignity. It surprised Thursdale to find what freshness of heart he brought to the adventure: and though his sense of irony prevented his ascribing his intactness to any conscious purpose, he could but rejoice in the fact that his sentimental economies had left him such a large surplus to draw upon.

Mrs. Vervain was at home—as usual. When one visits the cemetery one expects to find the angel on the tombstone, and it struck Thursdale as another proof of his friend's good taste that she had been in no undue haste to change her habits. The whole house appeared to count on his coming; the footman took his hat and overcoat as naturally as though there had been no lapse in his visits; and the drawing-room at once enveloped him in that at-mosphere of tacit intelligence which Mrs. Vervain imparted to her very furniture.

It was a surprise that, in this general harmony of circum-stances, Mrs. Vervain should herself sound the first false note.

"You?" she exclaimed; and the book she held slipped from her hand.

It was crude, certainly; unless it were a touch of the finest art. The difficulty of classifying it disturbed Thursdale's balance.

"Why not?" he said, restoring the book. "Isn't it my hour?" And as she made no answer, he added gently, "Unless it's some one else's?"

She laid the book aside and sank back into her chair. "Mine, merely," she said.

"I hope that doesn't mean that you're unwilling to share it?"

"With you? By no means. You're welcome to my last crust."

He looked at her reproachfully. "Do you call this the last?"

She smiled as he dropped into the seat across the hearth. "It's a way of giving it more flavour!"

He returned the smile. "A visit to you doesn't need such condiments."

She took this with just the right measure of retrospective amusement.

"Ah, but I want to put into this one a very special taste," she confessed.

Her smile was so confident, so reassuring, that it lulled him into the imprudence of saying: "Why should you want it to be different from what was always so perfectly right?"

She hesitated. "Doesn't the fact that it's the last constitute a dif-ference?"

"The last—my last visit to you?"

"Oh, metaphorically, I mean—there's a break in the con-tinuity."

Decidedly, she was pressing too hard: unlearning his arts already!

"I don't recognise it," he said. "Unless you make me—" he added, with a note that slightly stirred her attitude of languid attention.

She turned to him with grave eyes. "You recognise no difference whatever?"

"None—except an added link in the chain."

"An added link?"

"In having one more thing to like you for—your letting Miss Gaynor see why I had already so many." He flattered himself that this turn had taken the least hint of fatuity from the phrase.

Mrs. Vervain sank into her former easy pose. "Was it that you came for?" she asked, almost gaily.

"If it is necessary to have a reason—that was one."

"To talk to me about Miss Gaynor?"

"To tell you how she talks about you."

"That will be very interesting—especially if you have seen her since her second visit to me."

"Her second visit?" Thursdale pushed his chair back with a start and moved to another. "She came to see you again?"

"This morning, yes—by appointment."

He continued to look at her blankly. "You sent for her?"

"I didn't have to—she wrote and asked me last night. But no doubt you have seen her since."

Thursdale sat silent. He was trying to separate his words from his thoughts, but they still clung together inextricably. "I saw her off just now at the station."

"And she didn't tell you that she had been here again?"

"There was hardly time, I suppose—there were people about—" he floundered.

"Ah, she'll write, then."

He regained his composure. "Of course she'll write: very often, I hope. You know I'm absurdly in love," he cried audaciously.

She tilted her head back, looking up at him as he leaned against the chimney-piece. He had leaned there so often that the attitude touched a pulse which set up a throbbing in her throat. "Oh, my poor Thursdale!" she murmured.

"I suppose it's rather ridiculous," he owned; and as she remained silent, he added, with a sudden break—"Or have you another reason for pitying me?"

Her answer was another question. "Have you been back to your rooms since you left her?"

"Since I left her at the station? I came straight here."

"Ah, yes—you *could:* there was no reason—" Her words passed into a silent musing.

Thursdale moved nervously nearer. "You said you had something to tell me?"

"Perhaps I had better let her do so. There may be a letter at your rooms."

"A letter? What do you mean? A letter from *her*? What has happened?"

His paleness shook her, and she raised a hand of reassurance. "Nothing has happened—perhaps that is just the worst of it. You always *hated*, you know," she added incoherently, "to have things happen: you never would let them."

"And now—?"

"Well, that was what she came here for: I supposed you had guessed. To know if anything had happened."

"Had happened?" He gazed at her slowly. "Between you and me?" he said with a rush of light.

The words were so much cruder than any that had ever passed between them, that the colour rose to her face; but she held his startled gaze.

"You know girls are not quite as unsophisticated as they used to be. Are you surprised that such an idea should occur to her?"

His own colour answered hers: it was the only reply that came to him.

Mrs. Vervain went on smoothly: "I supposed it might have struck you that there were times when we presented that appearance."

He made an impatient gesture. "A man's past is his own!"

"Perhaps—it certainly never belongs to the woman who has shared it. But one learns such truths only by experience; and Miss Gaynor is naturally inexperienced."

"Of course—but—supposing her act a natural one—" he floundered lamentably among his innuendoes—"I still don't see—how there was anything—"

"Anything to take hold of? There wasn't—"

"Well, then—?" escaped him, in undisguised satisfaction; but as she did not complete the sentence he went on with a faltering laugh: "She can hardly object to the existence of a mere friendship between us!"

"But she does," said Mrs. Vervain.

Thursdale stood perplexed. He had seen, on the previous day, no trace of jealousy or resentment in his betrothed: he could still hear the candid ring of the girl's praise of Mrs. Vervain. If she were such an abyss of insincerity as to dissemble distrust under such frankness, she must at least be more subtle than to bring her doubts to her rival for solution. The situation seemed one through which one could no longer move in a penumbra, and he let in a burst of light with the direct query: "Won't you explain what you mean?"

Mrs. Vervain sat silent, not provokingly, as though to prolong his distress, but as if, in the attenuated phraseology he had taught her, it was difficult to find words robust enough to meet his challenge. It was the first time he had ever asked her to explain anything; and she had lived so long in dread of offering elucidations which were not wanted, that she seemed unable to produce one on the spot.

At last she said slowly: "She came to find out if you were really free."

Thursdale coloured again. "Free?" he stammered, with a sense of physical disgust at contact with such crassness.

"Yes—if I had quite done with you." She smiled in recovered security. "It seems she likes clear outlines; she has a passion for definitions."

"Yes—well?" he said, wincing at the echo of his own subtlety.

"Well—and when I told her that you had never belonged to me, she wanted me to define *my* status—to know exactly where I had stood all along."

Thursdale sat gazing at her intently; his hand was not yet on the clue. "And even when you had told her that—"

"Even when I had told her that I had had no status—that I had never stood anywhere, in any sense she meant," said Mrs. Vervain, slowly—"even then she wasn't satisfied, it seems."

He uttered an uneasy exclamation. "She didn't believe you, you mean?"

"I mean that she *did* believe me: too thoroughly."

"Well, then—in God's name, what did she want?"

"Something more—those were the words she used."

"Something more? Between—between you and me? Is it a conundrum?" He laughed awkwardly.

"Girls are not what they were in my day; they are no longer forbidden to contemplate the relation of the sexes."

"So it seems!" he commented. "But since, in this case, there wasn't any—" he broke off, catching the dawn of a revelation in her gaze.

"That's just it. The unpardonable offence has been—in our not offending."

He flung himself down despairingly. "I give it up!—What did you tell her?" he burst out with sudden crudeness.

"The exact truth. If I had only known," she broke off with a beseeching tenderness, "won't you believe that I would still have lied for you?"

"Lied for me? Why on earth should you have lied for either of us?"

"To save you—to hide you from her to the last! As I've hidden you from myself all these years!" She stood up with a sudden tragic import in her movement. "You believe me capable of that, don't you? If I had only guessed—but I have never known a girl like her; she had the truth out of me with a spring."

"The truth that you and I had never—"

"Had never—never in all these years! Oh, she knew why—she measured us both in a flash. She didn't suspect me of having haggled with you—her words pelted me like hail. 'He just took what he wanted—sifted and sorted you to suit his taste. Burnt out the gold and left a heap of cinders. And you let him—you let yourself be cut in bits'—she mixed her metaphors a little—'be cut in bits, and used or discarded, while all the while every drop of blood in you belonged to him! But he's Shylock—he's Shylock—and you have bled to death of the pound of flesh he has cut off you.' But she despises me the most, you know—far the most—" Mrs. Vervain ended.

The words fell strangely on the scented stillness of the room: they seemed out of harmony with its setting of afternoon intimacy, the kind of intimacy on which, at any moment, a visitor might intrude without perceptibly lowering the atmosphere. It was as though a grand opera-singer had strained the acoustics of a private music-room.

Thursdale stood up, facing his hostess. Half the room was between them, but they seemed to stare close at each other now that the veils of reticence and ambiguity had fallen.

His first words were characteristic: "She *does* despise me, then?" he exclaimed.

"She thinks the pound of flesh you took was a little too near the heart."

He was excessively pale. "Please tell me exactly what she said of me."

"She did not speak much of you: she is proud. But I gather that while she understands love or indifference, her eyes have never been opened to the many intermediate shades of feeling. At any rate, she expressed an unwillingness to be taken with reservations—she thinks you would have loved her better if you had loved some one else first. The point of view is original—she insists on a man with a past!"

"Oh, a past—if she's serious—I could rake up a past!" he said with a laugh.

"So I suggested: but she has her eyes on this particular portion of it. She insists on making it a test case. She wanted to know what you had done to me; and before I could guess her drift I blundered into telling her."

Thursdale drew a difficult breath. "I never supposed—your revenge is complete," he said slowly.

. He heard a little gasp in her throat. "My revenge? When I sent for you to warn you—to save you from being surprised as *I* was surprised?"

"You're very good—but it's rather late to talk of saving me." He held out his hand in the mechanical gesture of leave-taking.

"How you must care!—for I never saw you so dull," was her answer. "Don't you see that it's not too late for me to help you?" And as he continued to stare, she brought out sublimely: "Take the rest—in imagination! Let it at least be of that much use to you. Tell her I lied to her—she's too ready to believe it! And so, after all, in a sense, I sha'n't have been wasted."

His stare hung on her, widening to a kind of wonder. She gave the look back brightly, unblushingly, as though the expedient were too simple to need oblique approaches. It was extraordinary how a few words had swept them from an atmosphere of the most complex dissimulations to this contact of naked souls.

It was not in Thursdale to expand with the pressure of fate; but something in him cracked with it, and the rift let in new light. He went up to his friend and took her hand.

"You would do it—you would do it!"

She looked at him, smiling, but her hand shook.

"Good-bye," he said, kissing it.

"Good-bye? You are going—?"

"To get my letter."

"Your letter? The letter won't matter, if you will only do what I ask."

He returned her gaze. "I might, I suppose, without being out of character. Only, don't you see that if your plan helped me it could only harm her?"

"Harm *her*?"

"To sacrifice you wouldn't make me different. I shall go on being what I have always been—sifting and sorting, as she calls it. Do you want my punishment to fall on *her*?"

She looked at him long and deeply. "Ah, if I had to choose between you—!"

"You would let her take her chance? But I can't, you see. I must take my punishment alone."

She drew her hand away, sighing. "Oh, there will be no punishment for either of you."

"For either of us? There will be the reading of her letter for me."

She shook her head with a slight laugh. "There will be no letter."

Thursdale faced about from the threshold with fresh life in his look. "No letter? You don't mean—"

"I mean that she's been with you since I saw her—she's seen you and heard your voice. If there *is* a letter, she has recalled it—from the first station, by telegraph."

He turned back to the door, forcing an answer to her smile. "But in the meanwhile I shall have read it," he said.

The door closed on him, and she hid her eyes from the dreadful emptiness of the room.

. . .

XINGU

CHAPTER 1

Mrs. Ballinger is one of the ladies who pursue Culture in bands, as though it were dangerous to meet alone. To this end she had founded the Lunch Club, an association composed of herself and several other indomitable huntresses of erudition. The Lunch Club, after three or four winters of lunching and debate, had acquired such local distinction that the entertainment of distinguished strangers became one of its accepted functions; in recognition of which it duly extended to the celebrated "Osric Dane," on the day of her arrival in Hillbridge, an invitation to be present at the next meeting.

The club was to meet at Mrs. Ballinger's. The other members, behind her back, were of one voice in deploring her unwillingness to cede her rights in favor of Mrs. Plinth, whose house made a more impressive setting for the entertainment of celebrities; while, as Mrs. Leveret observed, there was always the picture-gallery to fall back on.

Mrs. Plinth made no secret of sharing this view. She had always regarded it as one of her obligations to entertain the Lunch Club's distinguished guests. Mrs. Plinth was almost as proud of her obligations as she was of her picture-gallery; she was in fact fond of implying that the one possession implied the other, and that only a woman of her wealth could afford to live up to a standard as high as that which she had set herself. An all-round sense of duty, roughly adaptable to various ends, was, in her opinion, all that Providence exacted of the more humbly stationed; but the power which had predestined Mrs. Plinth to keep a footman clearly intended her to maintain an equally specialized staff of responsibilities. It was the more to be regretted that Mrs. Ballinger, whose obligations to society were bounded by the narrow scope of two parlour-maids, should have been so tenacious of the right to entertain Osric Dane.

The question of that lady's reception had for a month past profoundly moved the members of the Lunch Club. It was not that they felt themselves unequal to the task, but that their sense of the opportunity plunged them into the agreeable uncertainty of the lady who weighs the alternatives of a well-stocked wardrobe. If such subsidiary members as Mrs. Leveret were fluttered by the thought of exchanging ideas with the author of "The Wings of Death," no forebodings disturbed the conscious adequacy of Mrs. Plinth, Mrs. Ballinger and Miss Van Vluyck. "The Wings of Death" had, in fact, at Miss Van Vluyck's suggestion, been chosen as the subject of discussion at the last club meeting, and each member had thus been enabled to express her own opinion or to appropriate whatever sounded well in the comments of the others.

Mrs. Roby alone had abstained from profiting by the opportunity; but it was now openly recognised that, as a member of the Lunch Club, Mrs. Roby was a failure. "It all comes," as Miss Van Vluyck put it, "of accepting a woman on a man's estimation." Mrs. Roby, returning to Hillbridge from a prolonged sojourn in exotic lands—the other ladies no longer took the trouble to remember where—had been heralded by the distinguished biologist, Professor Foreland, as the most agreeable woman he had ever met; and the members of the Lunch Club, impressed by an encomium that carried the weight of a diploma, and rashly assuming that the Professor's social sympathies would follow the line of his professional bent, had seized the chance of annexing a biological member. Their disillusionment was complete. At Miss Van Vluyck's first offhand mention of the pterodactyl Mrs. Roby had confusedly murmured: "I know so little about metres—" and after that painful betrayal of incompetence she had prudently withdrawn from farther participation in the mental gymnastics of the club.

"I suppose she flattered him," Miss Van Vluyck summed up— "or else it's the way she does her hair."

The dimensions of Miss Van Vluyck's dining-room having restricted the membership of the club to six, the non-conductiveness of one member was a serious obstacle to the exchange of ideas, and some wonder had already been expressed that Mrs. Roby should care to live, as it were, on the intellectual bounty of the others. This feeling was increased by the discovery that she had not yet read "The Wings of Death." She owned to having heard the name of Osric Dane; but that—incredible as it appeared—was the extent of her acquaintance with the celebrated novelist. The ladies could not conceal their surprise; but Mrs. Ballinger, whose pride in the club made her wish to put even Mrs. Roby in the best possible light, gently insinuated that, though she had not time to acquaint herself with "The Wings of Death," she must at least be familiar with its equally remarkable predecessor, "The Supreme Instant."

Mrs. Roby wrinkled her sunny brows in a conscientious effort of memory, as a result of which she recalled that, oh, yes, she *had* seen the book at her brother's, when she was staying with him in Brazil, and had even carried it off to read one day on a boating party; but they had all got to shying things at each other in the boat, and the book had gone overboard, so she had never had the chance—

The picture evoked by this anecdote did not increase Mrs. Roby's credit with the club, and there was a painful pause, which was broken by Mrs. Plinth's remarking: "I can understand that, with all your other pursuits, you should not find much time for reading; but I should have thought you might at least have *got up* 'The Wings of Death,' before Osric Dane's arrival."

Mrs. Roby took this rebuke good-humouredly. She had meant, she owned, to glance through the book; but she had been so absorbed in a novel of Trollope's that—

"No one reads Trollope now," Mrs. Ballinger interrupted.

Mrs. Roby looked pained. "I'm only just beginning," she confessed.

"And does he interest you?" Mrs. Plinth enquired.

"He amuses me."

"Amusement," said Mrs. Plinth, "is hardly what I look for in my choice of books."

"Oh, certainly, 'The Wings of Death' is not amusing," ventured Mrs. Leveret, whose manner of putting forth an opinion was like that of an obliging salesman with a variety of other styles to submit if his first selection does not suit.

"Was it *meant* to be?" enquired Mrs. Plinth, who was fond of asking questions that she permitted no one but herself to answer. "Assuredly not."

"Assuredly not—that is what I was going to say," assented Mrs. Leveret, hastily rolling up her opinion and reaching for another. "It was meant to—to elevate."

Miss Van Vluyck adjusted her spectacles as though they were the black cap of condemnation. "I hardly see," she interposed, "how a book steeped in the bitterest pessimism can be said to elevate, however much it may instruct."

"I meant, of course, to instruct," said Mrs. Leveret, flurried by the unexpected distinction between two terms which she had supposed to be synonymous. Mrs. Leveret's enjoyment of the Lunch Club was frequently marred by such surprises; and not knowing her own value to the other ladies as a mirror for their mental complacency she was sometimes troubled by a doubt of her worthiness to join in their debates. It was only the fact of having a dull sister who thought her clever that saved her from a sense of hopeless inferiority.

"Do they get married in the end?" Mrs. Roby interposed.

"They—who?" the Lunch Club collectively exclaimed.

"Why, the girl and man. It's a novel, isn't it? I always think that's the one thing that matters. If they're parted, it spoils my dinner."

Mrs. Plinth and Mrs. Ballinger exchanged scandalised glances, and the latter said: "I should hardly advise you to read 'The Wings of Death' in that spirit. For my part, when there are so many books one *has* to read, I wonder how any one can find time for those that are merely amusing."

"The beautiful part of it," Laura Glyde murmured, "is surely just this—that no one can tell *how* 'The Wings of Death' ends. Osric Dane, overcome by the awful significance of her own meaning, has mercifully veiled it—perhaps even from herself—as Apelles, in representing the sacrifice of Iphigenia, veiled the face of Agamemnon."

"What's that? Is it poetry?" whispered Mrs. Leveret to Mrs. Plinth, who, disdaining a definite reply, said coldly: "You should look it up. I always make it a point to look things up." Her tone added—"though I might easily have it done for me by the footman."

"I was about to say," Miss Van Vluyck resumed, "that it must always be a question whether a book *can* instruct unless it elevates."

"Oh—" murmured Mrs. Leveret, now feeling herself hopelessly astray.

"I don't know," said Mrs. Ballinger, scenting in Miss Van Vluyck's tone a tendency to depreciate the coveted distinction of entertaining Osric Dane; "I don't know that such a distinction can seriously be raised as to a book which has attracted more attention among thoughtful people than any novel since 'Robert Elsmere.'"

"Oh, but don't you see," exclaimed Laura Glyde, "that it's just the dark hopelessness of it all—the wonderful tone-scheme of black on black—that makes it such an artistic achievement? It reminded me when I read it of Prince Rupert's *manière noire* . . . the book is etched, not painted, yet one feels the colour-values so intensely. . . ."

"Who is *he*?" Mrs. Leveret whispered to her neighbour. "Some one she's met abroad?"

"The wonderful part of the book," Mrs. Ballinger conceded, "is that it may be looked at from so many points of view. I hear that as a study of determinism Professor Lupton ranks it with 'The Data of Ethics.'"

"I'm told that Osric Dane spent ten years in preparatory studies before beginning to write it," said Mrs. Plinth. "She looks up everything—verifies everything. It has always been my principle, as you know. Nothing would induce me, now, to put aside a book before I'd finished it, just because I can buy as many more as I want."

"And what do *you* think of 'The Wings of Death'?" Mrs. Roby abruptly asked her.

It was the kind of question that might be termed out of order, and the ladies glanced at each other as though disclaiming any share in such a breach of discipline. They all knew there was nothing Mrs. Plinth so much disliked as being asked her opinion of a book. Books were written to read; if one read them what more could be expected? To be questioned in detail regarding the contents of a volume seemed to her as great an outrage as being searched for smuggled laces at the Custom House. The club had always respected this idiosyncrasy of Mrs. Plinth's. Such opinions as she had were imposing and substantial: her mind, like her house, was furnished with monumental "pieces" that were not meant to be disarranged; and it was one of the unwritten rules of the Lunch Club that, within her own province, each member's habits of thought should be respected. The meeting therefore closed with an increased sense, on the part of the other ladies, of Mrs. Roby's hopeless unfitness to be one of them.

CHAPTER 2

Mrs. Leveret, on the eventful day, arrived early at Mrs. Ballinger's, her volume of Appropriate Allusions in her pocket.

It always flustered Mrs. Leveret to be late at the Lunch Club; she liked to collect her thoughts and gather a hint, as the others assembled, of the turn the conversation was likely to take. To-day, however, she felt herself completely at a loss; and even the familiar contact of Appropriate Allusions, which stuck into her as she sat down, failed to give her any reassurance. It was an admirable little volume, compiled to meet all the social emergencies; so that, whether on the occasion of Anniversaries, joyful or melancholy, (as the classification ran), of Banquets, social or municipal, or of Baptisms, Church of England or sectarian, its student need never be at a loss for a pertinent reference. Mrs. Leveret, though she had for years devoutly conned its pages, valued it, however, rather for its moral support than for its practical services; for though in the privacy of her own room she commanded an army of quotations, these invariably deserted her at the critical moment, and the only phrase she retained—*Canst thou draw out leviathan with a hook?*—was one she had never yet found occasion to apply.

To-day she felt that even the complete mastery of the volume would hardly have insured her self-possession; for she thought it probable that, even if she *did*, in some miraculous way, remember an Allusion, it would be only to find that Osric Dane used a different volume (Mrs. Leveret was convinced that literary people always carried them), and would consequently not recognise her quotations.

Mrs. Leveret's sense of being adrift was intensified by the appearance of Mrs. Ballinger's drawing-room. To a careless eye its aspect was unchanged; but those acquainted with Mrs. Ballinger's way of arranging her books would instantly have detected the marks of recent perturbation. Mrs. Ballinger's province, as a member of the Lunch Club, was the Book of the Day. On that, whatever it was, from a novel to a treatise on experimental psychology, she was confidently, authoritatively "up." What became of last year's books, or last week's even; what she did with the "subjects" she had previously professed with equal authority; no one had ever yet discovered. Her mind was an hotel where facts came and went like transient lodgers, without leaving their address behind, and frequently without paying for their board. It was Mrs. Ballinger's boast that she was "abreast with the Thought of the Day," and her pride that this advanced position should be expressed by the books on her table. These volumes, frequently renewed, and almost always damp from the press, bore names generally unfamiliar to Mrs. Leveret, and giving her, as she furtively scanned them, a disheartening glimpse of new fields of knowledge to be breathlessly traversed in Mrs. Ballinger's wake. But to-day a number of maturer-looking volumes were adroitly mingled with the *primeurs* of the press—Karl Marx jostled Professor Bergson, and the "Confessions of St. Augustine" lay beside the last work on "Mendelism"; so that even to Mrs. Leveret's fluttered perceptions it was clear that Mrs. Ballinger didn't in the least know what Osric Dane was likely to talk about, and had taken measures to be prepared for anything. Mrs. Leveret felt like a passenger on an ocean steamer who is told that there is no immediate danger, but that she had better put on her life-belt.

It was a relief to be roused from these forebodings by Miss Van Vluyck's arrival.

"Well, my dear," the new-comer briskly asked her hostess, "what subjects are we to discuss to-day."

Mrs. Ballinger was furtively replacing a volume of Wordsworth by a copy of Verlaine. "I hardly know," she said, somewhat nervously. "Perhaps we had better leave that to circumstances."

"Circumstances?" said Miss Van Vluyck dryly. "That means, I suppose, that Laura Glyde will take the floor as usual, and we shall be deluged with literature."

Philanthropy and statistics were Miss Van Vluyck's province, and she resented any tendency to divert their guest's attention from these topics.

Mrs. Plinth at this moment appeared.

"Literature?" she protested in a tone of remonstrance. "But this is perfectly unexpected. I understood we were to talk of Osric Dane's novel."

Mrs. Ballinger winced at the discrimination, but let it pass. "We can hardly make that our chief subject—at least not *too* intentionally," she suggested. "Of course we can let our talk *drift* in that direction; but we ought to have some other topic as an introduction, and that is what I wanted to consult you about. The fact is, we know so little of Osric Dane's tastes and interests that it is difficult to make any special preparation."

"It may be difficult," said Mrs. Plinth with decision, "but it is necessary. I know what that happy-go-lucky principle leads to. As I told one of my nieces the other day, there are certain emergencies for which a lady should always be prepared. It's in shocking taste to wear colours when one pays a visit of condolence, or a last year's dress when there are reports that one's husband is on the wrong side of the market; and so it is with conversation. All I ask is that I should know beforehand what is to be talked about; then I feel sure of being able to say the proper thing."

"I quite agree with you," Mrs. Ballinger assented; "but—"

And at that instant, heralded by the fluttered parlour-maid, Osric Dane appeared upon the threshold.

Mrs. Leveret told her sister afterward that she had known at a glance what was coming. She saw that Osric Dane was not going to meet them half way. That distinguished personage had indeed entered with an air of compulsion not calculated to promote the easy exercise of hospitality. She looked as though she were about to be photographed for a new edition of her books.

The desire to propitiate a divinity is generally in inverse ratio to its responsiveness, and the sense of discouragement produced by Osric Dane's entrance visibly increased the Lunch Club's eagerness to please her. Any lingering idea that she might consider herself under an obligation to her entertainers was at once dispelled by her manner; as Mrs. Leveret said afterward to her sister, she had a way of looking at you that made you feel as if there was something wrong with your hat. This evidence of greatness produced such an immediate impression on the ladies that a shudder of awe ran through them when Mrs. Roby, as their hostess led the great personage into the dining-room, turned back to whisper to the others: "What a brute she is!"

The hour about the table did not tend to revise this verdict. It was passed by Osric Dane in the silent deglutition of Mrs. Ballinger's menu, and by the members of the club in the emission of tentative platitudes which their guest seemed to swallow as perfunctorily as the successive courses of the luncheon.

Mrs. Ballinger's reluctance to fix a topic had thrown the club into a mental disarray which increased with the return to the drawing-room, where the actual business of discussion was to open. Each lady waited for the other to speak; and there was a general shock of disappointment when their hostess opened the conversation by the painfully commonplace enquiry: "Is this your first visit to Hillbridge?"

Even Mrs. Leveret was conscious that this was a bad beginning; and a vague impulse of deprecation made Miss Glyde interject: "It is a very small place indeed."

Mrs. Plinth bristled. "We have a great many representative people," she said, in the tone of one who speaks for her order.

Osric Dane turned to her. "What do they represent?" she asked.

Mrs. Plinth's constitutional dislike to being questioned was intensified by her sense of unpreparedness; and her reproachful glance passed the question on to Mrs. Ballinger.

"Why," said that lady, glancing in turn at the other members, "as a community I hope it is not too much to say that we stand for culture."

"For art—" Miss Glyde interjected.

"For art and literature," Mrs. Ballinger emended.

"And for sociology, I trust," snapped Miss Van Vluyck.

"We have a standard," said Mrs. Plinth, feeling herself suddenly secure on the vast expanse of a generalisation; and Mrs. Leveret, thinking there must be room for more than one on so broad a statement, took courage to murmur: "Oh, certainly; we have a standard."

"The object of our little club," Mrs. Ballinger continued, "is to concentrate the highest tendencies of Hillbridge—to centralise and focus its intellectual effort."

This was felt to be so happy that the ladies drew an almost audible breath of relief.

"We aspire," the President went on, "to be in touch with whatever is highest in art, literature and ethics."

Osric Dane again turned to her. "What ethics?" she asked.

A tremor of apprehension encircled the room. None of the ladies required any preparation to pronounce on a question of morals; but when they were called ethics they were different. The club, when fresh from the "Encyclopædia Britannica," the "Reader's Handbook" or Smith's "Classical Dictionary," could deal confidently with any subject; but when taken unawares it had been known to define agnosticism as a heresy of the Early Church and Professor Froude as a distinguished histologist; and such minor members as Mrs. Leveret still secretly regarding ethics as something vaguely pagan.

Even to Mrs. Ballinger, Osric Dane's question was unsettling, and there was a general sense of gratitude when Laura Glyde leaned forward to say, with her most sympathetic accent: "You must excuse us, Mrs. Dane, for not being able, just at present, to talk of anything but 'The Wings of Death.'"

"Yes," Miss Van Vluyck, with a sudden resolve to carry the war into the enemy's camp. "We are so anxious to know the exact purpose you had in mind in writing your wonderful book."

"You will find," Mrs. Plinth interposed, "that we are not superficial readers."

"We are eager to hear from you," Miss Van Vluyck continued, "if the pessimistic tendency of the book is an expression of your own convictions or—"

"Or merely," Miss Glyde thrust in, "a sombre background brushed in to throw your figures into more vivid relief. *Are* you not primarily plastic?"

"*I* have always maintained," Mrs. Ballinger interposed, "that you represent the purely objective method—"

Osric Dane helped herself critically to coffee. "How do you define objective?" she then enquired.

There was a flurried pause before Laura Glyde intensely murmured: "In reading *you* we don't define, we feel."

Osric Dane smiled. "The cerebellum," she remarked, "is not infrequently the seat of the literary emotions." And she took a second lump of sugar.

The sting that this remark was vaguely felt to conceal was almost neutralised by the satisfaction of being addressed in such technical language.

"Ah, the cerebellum," said Miss Van Vluyck complacently. "The club took a course in psychology last winter."

"Which psychology?" asked Osric Dane.

There was an agonising pause, during which each member of the club secretly deplored the distressing inefficiency of the others. Only Mrs. Roby went on placidly sipping her chartreuse. At last Mrs. Ballinger said, with an attempt at a high tone: "Well, really, you know, it was last year that we took psychology, and this winter we have been so absorbed in—"

She broke off, nervously trying to recall some of the club's discussions; but her faculties seemed to be paralysed by the petrifying stare of Osric Dane. What *had* the club been absorbed in? Mrs. Ballinger, with a vague purpose of gaining time, repeated slowly: "We've been so intensely absorbed in—"

Mrs. Roby put down her liqueur glass and drew near the group with a smile.

"In Xingu?" she gently prompted.

A thrill ran through the other members. They exchanged confused glances, and then, with one accord, turned a gaze of mingled relief and interrogation on their rescuer. The expression of each denoted a different phase of the same emotion. Mrs. Plinth was the first to compose her features to an air of reassurance: after a moment's hasty adjustment her look almost implied that it was she who had given the word to Mrs. Ballinger.

"Xingu, of course!" exclaimed the latter with her accustomed promptness, while Miss Van Vluyck and Laura Glyde seemed to be plumbing the depths of memory, and Mrs. Leveret, feeling apprehensively for Appropriate Allusions, was somehow reassured by the uncomfortable pressure of its bulk against her person.

Osric Dane's change of countenance was no less striking than that of her entertainers. She too put down her coffee-cup, but with a look of distinct annoyance; she too wore, for a brief moment, what Mrs. Roby afterward described as the look of feeling for something in the back of her head; and before she could dissemble these momentary signs of weakness, Mrs. Roby, turning to her with a deferential smile, had said: "And we've been so hoping that to-day you would tell us just what you think of it."

Osric Dane received the homage of the smile as a matter of course; but the accompanying question obviously embarrassed her, and it became clear to her observers that she was not quick at shifting her facial scenery. It was as though her countenance had so long been set in an expression of unchallenged superiority that the muscles had stiffened, and refused to obey her orders.

"Xingu—" she said, as if seeking in her turn to gain time.

Mrs. Roby continued to press her. "Knowing how engrossing the subject is, you will understand how it happens that the club has let everything else go to the wall for the moment. Since we took up Xingu I might almost say—were it not for your books— that nothing else seems to us worth remembering."

Osric Dane's stern features were darkened rather than lit up by an uneasy smile. "I am glad to hear that you make one exception," she gave out between narrowed lips.

"Oh, of course," Mrs. Roby said prettily; "but as you have shown us that—so very naturally!—you don't care to talk of your own things, we really can't let you off from telling us exactly what you think about Xingu; especially," she added, with a still more persuasive smile, "as some people say that one of your last books was saturated with it."

It was an *it*, then—the assurance sped like fire through the parched minds of the other members. In their eagerness to gain the least little clue to Xingu they almost forgot the joy of assisting at the discomfiture of Mrs. Dane.

The latter reddened nervously under her antagonist's challenge. "May I ask," she faltered out, "to which of my books you refer?"

Mrs. Roby did not falter. "That's just what I want you to tell us; because, though I was present, I didn't actually take part."

"Present at what?" Mrs. Dane took her up; and for an instant the trembling members of the Lunch Club thought that the champion Providence had raised up for them had lost a point. But Mrs. Roby explained herself gaily: "At the discussion, of course. And so we're dreadfully anxious to know just how it was that you went into the Xingu."

There was a portentous pause, a silence so big with incalculable dangers that the members with one accord checked the words on their lips, like soldiers dropping their arms to watch a single combat between their leaders. Then Mrs. Dane gave expression to their inmost dread by saying sharply: "Ah—you say *the* Xingu, do you?"

Mrs. Roby smiled undauntedly. "It *is* a shade pedantic, isn't it? Personally, I always drop the article; but I don't know how the other members feel about it."

The other members looked as though they would willingly have dispensed with this appeal to their opinion, and Mrs. Roby, after a bright glance about the group, went on: "They probably think, as I do, that nothing really matters except the thing itself—except Xingu."

No immediate reply seemed to occur to Mrs. Dane, and Mrs. Ballinger gathered courage to say: "Surely every one must feel that about Xingu."

Mrs. Plinth came to her support with a heavy murmur of assent, and Laura Glyde sighed out emotionally: "I have known cases where it has changed a whole life."

"It has done me worlds of good," Mrs. Leveret interjected, seeming to herself to remember that she had either taken it or read it the winter before.

"Of course," Mrs. Roby admitted, "the difficulty is that one must give up so much time to it. It's very long."

"I can't imagine," said Miss Van Vluyck, "grudging the time given to such a subject."

"And deep in places," Mrs. Roby pursued; (so then it was a book!) "And it isn't easy to skip."

"I never skip," said Mrs. Plinth dogmatically.

"Ah, it's dangerous to, in Xingu. Even at the start there are places where one can't. One must just wade through."

"I should hardly call it *wading*," said Mrs. Ballinger sarcastically.

Mrs. Roby sent her a look of interest. "Ah—you always found it went swimmingly?"

Mrs. Ballinger hesitated. "Of course there are difficult passages," she conceded.

"Yes; some are not at all clear—even," Mrs. Roby added, "if one is familiar with the original."

"As I suppose you are?" Osric Dane interposed, suddenly fixing her with a look of challenge.

Mrs. Roby met it by a deprecating gesture. "Oh, it's really not difficult up to a certain point; though some of the branches are very little known, and it's almost impossible to get at the source."

"Have you ever tried?" Mrs. Plinth enquired, still distrustful of Mrs. Roby's thoroughness.

Mrs. Roby was silent for a moment; then she replied with lowered lids: "No—but a friend of mine did; a very brilliant man; and he told me it was best for women—not to. . . ."

A shudder ran around the room. Mrs. Leveret coughed so that the parlour-maid, who was handing the cigarettes, should not hear; Miss Van Vluyck's face took on a nauseated expression, and Mrs. Plinth looked as if she were passing some one she did not care to bow to. But the most remarkable result of Mrs. Roby's words was the effect they produced on the Lunch Club's distinguished guest. Osric Dane's impassive features suddenly softened to an expression of the warmest human sympathy, and edging her chair toward Mrs. Roby's she asked: "Did he really? And—did you find he was right?"

Mrs. Ballinger, in whom annoyance at Mrs. Roby's unwonted assumption of prominence was beginning to displace gratitude for the aid she had rendered, could not consent to her being allowed, by such dubious means, to monopolise the attention of their guest. If Osric Dane had not enough self-respect to resent Mrs. Roby's flippancy, at least the Lunch Club would do so in the person of its President.

Mrs. Ballinger laid her hand on Mrs. Roby's arm. "We must not forget," she said with a frigid amiability, "that absorbing as Xingu is to *us*, it may be less interesting to—"

"Oh, no, on the contrary, I assure you," Osric Dane intervened.

"—to others," Mrs. Ballinger finished firmly; "and we must not allow our little meeting to end without persuading Mrs. Dane to say a few words to us on a subject which, to-day, is much more present in all our thoughts. I refer, of course, to 'The Wings of Death.'"

The other members, animated by various degrees of the same sentiment, and encouraged by the humanised mien of their redoubtable guest, repeated after Mrs. Ballinger: "Oh, yes, you really *must* talk to us a little about your book."

Osric Dane's expression became as bored, though not as haughty, as when her work had been previously mentioned. But before she could respond to Mrs. Ballinger's request, Mrs. Roby had risen from her seat, and was pulling down her veil over her frivolous nose.

"I'm so sorry," she said, advancing toward her hostess with outstretched hand, "but before Mrs. Dane begins I think I'd better run away. Unluckily, as you know, I haven't read her books, so I should be at a terrible disadvantage among you all, and besides, I've an engagement to play bridge."

If Mrs. Roby had simply pleaded her ignorance of Osric Dane's works as a reason for withdrawing, the Lunch Club, in view of her recent prowess, might have approved such evidence of discretion; but to couple this excuse with the brazen announcement that she was foregoing the privilege for the purpose of joining a bridge-party was only one more instance of her deplorable lack of discrimination.

The ladies were disposed, however, to feel that her departure—now that she had performed the sole service she was ever likely to render them—would probably make for greater order and dignity in the impending discussion, besides relieving them of the sense of self-distrust which her presence always mysteriously produced. Mrs. Ballinger therefore restricted herself to a formal murmur of regret, and the other members were just grouping themselves comfortably about Osric Dane when the latter, to their dismay, started up from the sofa on which she had been seated.

"Oh wait—do wait, and I'll go with you!" she called out to Mrs. Roby; and, seizing the hands of the disconcerted members, she administered a series of farewell pressures with the mechanical haste of a railway-conductor punching tickets.

"I'm so sorry—I'd quite forgotten—" she flung back at them from the threshold; and as she joined Mrs. Roby, who had turned

in surprise at her appeal, the other ladies had the mortification of
hearing her say, in a voice which she did not take pains to lower:
"If you'll let me walk a little way with you, I should so like to ask
you a few more questions about Xingu . . ."

CHAPTER 3

The incident had been so rapid that the door closed on the
departing pair before the other members had time to understand
what was happening. Then a sense of the indignity put upon
them by Osric Dane's unceremonious desertion began to contend
with the confused feeling that they had been cheated out of their
due without exactly knowing how or why.

There was a silence, during which Mrs. Ballinger, with a perfunctory hand, rearranged the skilfully grouped literature at
which her distinguished guest had not so much as glanced; then
Miss Van Vluyck tartly pronounced: "Well, I can't say that I consider Osric Dane's departure a great loss."

This confession crystallised the resentment of the other members, and Mrs. Leveret exclaimed: "I do believe she came on
purpose to be nasty!"

It was Mrs. Plinth's private opinion that Osric Dane's attitude
toward the Lunch Club might have been very different had it welcomed her in the majestic setting of the Plinth drawing-rooms;
but not liking to reflect on the inadequacy of Mrs. Ballinger's
establishment she sought a roundabout satisfaction in depreciat-
ing her lack of foresight.

"I said from the first that we ought to have had a subject ready.
It's what always happens when you're unprepared. Now if we'd
only got up Xingu—"

The slowness of Mrs. Plinth's mental processes was always
allowed for by the club; but this instance of it was too much for
Mrs. Ballinger's equanimity.

"Xingu!" she scoffed. "Why, it was the fact of our knowing so

much more about it then she did—unprepared though we were—
that made Osric Dane so furious. I should have thought that was
plain enough to everybody!"

This retort impressed even Mrs. Plinth, and Laura Glyde,
moved by an impulse of generosity, said: "Yes, we really ought to
be grateful to Mrs. Roby for introducing the topic. It may have
made Osric Dane furious, but at least it made her civil."

"I am glad we were able to show her," added Miss Van Vluyck,
"that a broad and up-to-date culture is not confined to the great
intellectual centres."

This increased the satisfaction of the other members, and they
began to forget their wrath against Osric Dane in the pleasure of
having contributed to her discomfiture.

Miss Van Vluyck thoughtfully rubbed her spectacles. "What
surprised me most," she continued, "was that Fanny Roby should
be so up on Xingu."

This remark threw a slight chill on the company, but Mrs.
Ballinger said with an air of indulgent irony: "Mrs. Roby always
has the knack of making a little go a long way; still, we certainly
owe her a debt for happening to remember that she'd heard of
Xingu." And this was felt by the other members to be a graceful
way of cancelling once for all the club's obligation to Mrs. Roby.

Even Mrs. Leveret took courage to speed a timid shaft of irony.
"I fancy Osric Dane hardly expected to take a lesson in Xingu at
Hillbridge!"

Mrs. Ballinger smiled. "When she asked me what we represented—do you remember?—I wish I'd simply said we represented
Xingu!"

All the ladies laughed appreciatively at this sally, except Mrs.
Plinth, who said, after a moment's deliberation: "I'm not sure it
would have been wise to do so."

Mrs. Ballinger, who was already beginning to feel as if she had
launched at Osric Dane the retort which had just occurred to her,
turned ironically on Mrs. Plinth. "May I ask why?" she enquired.

Mrs. Plinth looked grave. "Surely," she said, "I understood

from Mrs. Roby herself that the subject was one it was as well not to go into too deeply?"

Miss Van Vluyck rejoined with precision: "I think that applied only to an investigation of the origin of the—of the—"; and suddenly she found that her usually accurate memory had failed her. "It's a part of the subject I never studied myself," she concluded.

"Nor I," said Mrs. Ballinger.

Laura Glyde bent toward them with widened eyes. "And yet it seems—doesn't it?—the part that is fullest of an esoteric fascination?"

"I don't know on what you base that," said Miss Van Vluyck argumentatively.

"Well, didn't you notice how intensely interested Osric Dane became as soon as she heard what the brilliant foreigner—he *was* a foreigner, wasn't he?—had told Mrs. Roby about the origin—the origin of the rite—or whatever you call it?"

Mrs. Plinth looked disapproving, and Mrs. Ballinger visibly wavered. Then she said: "It may not be desirable to touch on the—on that part of the subject in general conversation; but, from the importance it evidently has to a woman of Osric Dane's distinction, I feel as if we ought not to be afraid to discuss it among ourselves—without gloves—though with closed doors, if necessary."

"I'm quite of your opinion," Miss Van Vluyck came briskly to her support; "on condition, that is, that all grossness of language is avoided."

"Oh, I'm sure we shall understand without that," Mrs. Leveret tittered; and Laura Glyde added significantly: "I fancy we can read between the lines," while Mrs. Ballinger rose to assure herself that the doors were really closed.

Mrs. Plinth had not yet given her adhesion. "I hardly see," she began, "what benefit is to be derived from investigating such peculiar customs—"

But Mrs. Ballinger's patience had reached the extreme limit of tension. "This at least," she returned; "that we shall not be placed again in the humiliating position of finding ourselves less up on our own subjects than Fanny Roby!"

Even to Mrs. Plinth this argument was conclusive. She peered furtively about the room and lowered her commanding tones to ask: "Have you got a copy?"

"A—a copy?" stammered Mrs. Ballinger. She was aware that the other members were looking at her expectantly, and that this answer was inadequate, so she supported it by asking another question. "A copy of what?"

Her companions bent their expectant gaze on Mrs. Plinth, who, in turn, appeared less sure of herself than usual. "Why, of—of—the book," she explained.

"What book?" snapped Miss Van Vluyck, almost as sharply as Osric Dane.

Mrs. Ballinger looked at Laura Glyde, whose eyes were interrogatively fixed on Mrs. Leveret. The fact of being deferred to was so new to the latter that it filled her with an insane temerity. "Why, Xingu, of course!" she exclaimed.

A profound silence followed this challenge to the resources of Mrs. Ballinger's library, and the latter, after glancing nervously toward the Books of the Day, returned with dignity: "It's not a thing one cares to leave about."

"I should think *not*!" exclaimed Mrs. Plinth.

"It *is* as book, then?" said Miss Van Vluyck.

This again threw the company into disarray, and Mrs. Ballinger, with an impatient sigh, rejoined: "Why—there *is* a book—naturally. . . ."

"Then why did Miss Glyde call it a religion?"

Laura Glyde started up. "A religion? I never—"

"Yes, you did," Miss Van Vluyck insisted; "you spoke of rites; and Mrs. Plinth said it was a custom."

Miss Glyde was evidently making a desperate effort to recall her statement; but accuracy of detail was not her strongest point. At length she began in a deep murmur: "Surely they used to do something of the kind at the Eleusinian mysteries—"

"Oh—" said Miss Van Vluyck, on the verge of disapproval; and Mrs. Plinth protested: "I understood there was to be no indelicacy!"

Mrs. Ballinger could not control her irritation. "Really, it is too bad that we should not be able to talk the matter over quietly among ourselves. Personally, I think that if one goes into Xingu at all—"

"Oh, so do I!" cried Miss Glyde.

"And I don't see how one can avoid doing so, if one wishes to keep up with the Thought of the Day—"

Mrs. Leveret uttered an exclamation of relief. "There—that's it!" she interposed.

"What's it?" the President took her up.

"Why—it's a—a Thought: I mean a philosophy."

This seemed to bring a certain relief to Mrs. Ballinger and Laura Glyde, but Miss Van Vluyck said: "Excuse me if I tell you that you're all mistaken. Xingu happens to be a language."

"A language!" the Lunch Club cried.

"Certainly. Don't you remember Fanny Roby's saying that there were several branches, and that some were hard to trace? What could that apply to but dialects?"

Mrs. Ballinger could no longer restrain a contemptuous laugh. "Really, if the Lunch Club has reached such a pass that it has to go to Fanny Roby for instruction on a subject like Xingu, it had almost better cease to exist!"

"It's really her fault for not being clearer," Laura Glyde put in.

"Oh, clearness and Fanny Roby!" Mrs. Ballinger shrugged. "I daresay we shall find she was mistaken on almost every point."

"Why not look it up?" said Mrs. Plinth.

As a rule this recurrent suggestion of Mrs. Plinth's was ignored in the heat of discussion, and only resorted to afterward in the privacy of each member's home. But on the present occasion the desire to ascribe their own confusion of thought to the vague and contradictory nature of Mrs. Roby's statements caused the members of the Lunch Club to utter a collective demand for a book of reference.

At this point the production of her treasured volume gave Mrs. Leveret, for a moment, the unusual experience of occupying the centre front; but she was not able to hold it long, for Appropriate Allusions contained no reference of Xingu.

"Oh, that's not the kind of thing we want!" exclaimed Miss Van Vluyck. She cast a disparaging glance over Mrs. Ballinger's assortment of literature, and added impatiently: "Haven't you any useful books?"

"Of course I have," replied Mrs. Ballinger indignantly; "I keep them in my husband's dressing-room."

From this region, after some difficulty and delay, the parlour-maid produced the W-Z volume of an Encyclopædia and, in deference to the fact that the demand for it had come from Miss Van Vluyck, laid the ponderous tome before her.

There was a moment of painful suspense while Miss Van Vluyck rubbed her spectacles, adjusted them, and turned to Z; and a murmur of surprise when she said: "It isn't here."

"I suppose," said Mrs. Plinth, "it's not fit to be put in a book of reference."

"Oh, nonsense!" exclaimed Mrs. Ballinger. "Try X."

Miss Van Vluyck turned back through the volume, peering short-sightedly up and down the pages, till she came to a stop and remained motionless, like a dog on a point.

"Well, have you found it?" Mrs. Ballinger enquired after a considerable delay.

"Yes. I've found it," said Miss Van Vluyck in a queer voice.

Mrs. Plinth hastily interposed: "I beg you won't read it aloud if there's anything offensive."

Miss Van Vluyck, without answering, continued her silent scrutiny.

"Well, what *is* it?" exclaimed Laura Glyde excitedly.

"*Do* tell us!" urged Mrs. Leveret, feeling that she would have something awful to tell her sister.

Miss Van Vluyck pushed the volume aside and turned slowly toward the expectant group.

"It's a river."

"A *river*?"

"Yes: in Brazil. Isn't that where she's been living?"

"Who? Fanny Roby? Oh, but you must be mistaken. You've been reading the wrong thing," Mrs. Ballinger exclaimed, leaning over her to seize the volume.

"It's the only *Xingu* in the Encyclopædia; and she *has* been living in Brazil," Miss Van Vluyck persisted.

"Yes: her brother has a consulship there," Mrs. Leveret interposed.

"But it's too ridiculous! I—we—why we *all* remember studying Xingu last year—or the year before last," Mrs. Ballinger stammered.

"I thought I did when *you* said so," Laura Glyde avowed.

"*I* said so?" cried Mrs. Ballinger.

"Yes. You said it had crowded everything else out of your mind."

"Well *you* said it had changed your whole life!"

"For that matter, Miss Van Vluyck said she had never grudged the time she'd given it."

Mrs. Plinth interposed: "I made it clear that I knew nothing whatever of the original."

Mrs. Ballinger broke off the dispute with a groan. "Oh, what does it all matter if she's been making fools of us? I believe Miss Van Vluyck's right—she was talking of the river all the while!"

"How could she? It's too preposterous," Miss Glyde exclaimed.

"Listen." Miss Van Vluyck had repossessed herself of the Encyclopædia, and restored her spectacles to a nose reddened by excitement. "'The Xingu, one of the principal rivers of Brazil, rises on the plateau of Mato Grosso, and flows in a northerly direction for a length of no less than one thousand one hundred and eighteen miles, entering the Amazon near the mouth of the latter river. The upper course of the Xingu is auriferous and fed by numerous branches. Its source was first discovered in 1884 by the German explorer von den Steinen, after a difficult and dangerous expedition through a region inhabited by tribes still in the Stone Age of culture.'"

The ladies received this communication in a state of stupefied silence from which Mrs. Leveret was the first to rally. "She certainly *did* speak of it's having branches."

The word seemed to snap the last thread of their incredulity. "And of its great length," gasped Mrs. Ballinger.

"She said it was awfully deep, and you couldn't skip—you just had to wade through," Miss Glyde added.

The idea worked its way more slowly through Mrs. Plinth's compact resistances. "How could there be anything improper about a river?" she enquired.

"Improper?"

"Why, what she said about the source—that it was corrupt?"

"Not corrupt, but hard to get at," Laura Glyde corrected. "Some one who'd been there had told her so. I daresay it was the explorer himself—doesn't it say the expedition was dangerous?"

"'Difficult and dangerous,'" read Miss Van Vluyck.

Mrs. Ballinger pressed her hands to her throbbing temples. "There's nothing she said that wouldn't apply to a river—to this river!" She swung about excitedly to the other members. "Why, so you remember her telling us that she hadn't read 'The Supreme Instant' because she'd taken it on a boating party while she was staying with her brother, and some one had 'shied' it overboard—'shied' of course was her own expression."

The ladies breathlessly signified that the expression had not escaped them.

"Well—and then didn't she tell Osric Dane that one of her books was simply saturated with Xingu? Of course it was, if one of Mrs. Roby's rowdy friends had thrown it into the river!"

This surprising reconstruction of the scene in which they had just participated left the members of the Lunch Club inarticulate. At length, Mrs. Plinth, after visibly labouring with the problem, said in a heavy tone: "Osric Dane was taken in too."

Mrs. Leveret took courage at this. "Perhaps that's what Mrs. Roby did it for. She said Osric Dane was a brute, and she may have wanted to give her a lesson."

Miss Van Vluyck frowned. "It was hardly worth while to do it at our expense."

"At least," said Miss Glyde with a touch of bitterness, "she succeeded in interesting her, which was more than we did."

"What chance had we?" rejoined Mrs. Ballinger. "Mrs. Roby monopolised her from the first. And *that*, I've no doubt, was her purpose—to give Osric Dane a false impression of her own standing in the club. She would hesitate at nothing to attract attention; we all know how she took in poor Professor Foreland."

"She actually makes him give bridge-teas every Thursday," Mrs. Leveret piped up.

Laura Glyde struck her hands together. "Why, this is Thursday, and it's *there* she's gone, of course; and taken Osric with her!"

"And they're shrieking over us at this moment," said Mrs. Ballinger between her teeth.

This possibility seemed too preposterous to be admitted. "She would hardly dare," said Miss Van Vluyck, "confess the imposture to Osric Dane."

"I'm not so sure: I thought I saw her make a sign as she left. If she hadn't made a sign, why should Osric Dane have rushed out after her?"

"Well, you know, we'd all been telling her how wonderful Xingu was, and she wanted to find out more about it," Mrs. Leveret said, with a tardy impulse of justice to the absent.

This reminder, far from mitigating the wrath of the other members, gave it a stronger impetus.

"Yes—and that's exactly what they're both laughing over now," said Laura Glyde ironically.

Mrs. Plinth stood up and gathered her expensive furs about her monumental form. "I have no wish to criticise," she said; "but unless the Lunch Club can protect its members against the recurrence of such—such unbecoming scenes, I for one—"

"Oh, so do I!" agreed Miss Glyde, rising also.

Miss Van Vluyck closed the Encyclopædia and proceeded to button herself into her jacket. "My time is really too valuable—" she began.

"I fancy we are all of one mind," said Mrs. Ballinger, looking searchingly at Mrs. Leveret, who looked at the others.

"I always deprecate anything like a scandal—" Mrs. Plinth continued.

"She has been the cause of one to-day!" exclaimed Miss Glyde.

Mrs. Leveret moaned: "I don't see how she *could!*" and Miss Van Vluyck said, picking up her note-book: "Some women stop at nothing."

"—but if," Mrs. Plinth took up her argument impressively, "anything of the kind had happened in *my* house" (it never would have, her tone implied), "I should have felt that I owed it to myself either to ask for Mrs. Roby's resignation—or to offer mine."

"Oh, Mrs. Plinth—" gasped the Lunch Club.

"Fortunately for me," Mrs. Plinth continued with an awful magnanimity, "the matter was taken out of my hands by our President's decision that the right to entertain distinguished guests was a privilege vested in her office; and I think the other members will agree that, as she was alone in this opinion, she ought to be alone in deciding on the best way of effacing its—its really deplorable consequences."

A deep silence followed this outbreak of Mrs. Plinth's long-stored resentment.

"I don't see why *I* should be expected to ask her to resign—" Mrs. Ballinger at length began; but Laura Glyde turned back to remind her: "You know she made you say that you'd got on swimmingly in Xingu."

An ill-timed giggle escaped from Mrs. Leveret, and Mrs. Ballinger energetically continued "—but you needn't think for a moment that I'm afraid to!"

The door of the drawing-room closed on the retreating backs of the Lunch Club, and the President of that distinguished association, seating herself at her writing-table, and pushing away a copy of "The Wings of Death" to make room for her elbow, drew forth a sheet of the club's note-paper, on which she began to write: "My dear Mrs. Roby—"

. . .

ESSAY

From the Introduction to
Modern Critical Views: Edith Wharton

BY

HAROLD BLOOM

I

The most formidable figure in all Wallace Stevens's marvelous roster of fabulistic caricatures is that grand reductionist, "Mrs. Alfred Uruguay":

> So what said the others and the sun went down
> And, in the brown blues of evening, the lady said,
> In the donkey's ear, "I fear that elegance
> Must struggle like the rest." She climbed until
> The moonlight in her lap, mewing her velvet,
> And her dress were one and she said, "I have said no
> To everything, in order to get at myself.
> I have wiped away moonlight like mud. Your innocent ear
> And I, if I rode naked, are what remain."

Not for a moment do I suggest that this is an imaginary portrait of the formidable novelist Mrs. Edith Wharton, for Edith Wharton was more than a reductionist. Rather, Stevens's Mrs. Uruguay is a fierce reductionist out of old New York society as Wharton herself might have represented such a personage, and sometimes did. By "reductionist" I mean an adept in practicing what might be called "the reductive fallacy," which is the incessant translation of: "Tell me what she or he is *really* like," as: "Tell me the very worst thing you can, about her or him, which is in any way true or accurate."

Wharton's most savage portrait of such a reductionist is Undine Spragg in *The Custom of the Country*, which is likely to seem, some day, Wharton's strongest achievement, though I find it rather an unpleasant novel to reread. Undine Spragg (marvelous name! but then, Wharton's names are always superb) is not quite of the eminence of Thackeray's Becky Sharp, but she has an antithetical greatness about her that R. W. B. Lewis, Wharton's biographer, shrewdly traces to Wharton's dialectical self-knowledge:

> But the most of Edith Wharton is revealed, quite startlingly, in the characterization of Undine Spragg. No one (except possibly Ethan Frome) would at first glance seem more remote from Edith Wharton than Undine: a crude, unlettered, humorless, artificial, but exceedingly beautiful creature, with the most minimal moral intuitions and virtually no talent whatever for normal human affection. Undine did, undoubtedly, stand for everything in the new American female that Edith despised and recoiled from, But the matter, as it turns out, is much more interesting than that.
>
> There are smaller and larger telltale similarities. As a child Undine, like Edith, enjoyed dressing up in her mother's best finery and "playing lady" before a mirror. Moffatt addresses her by Edith's youthful nickname, "Puss." Edith's long yearning for psychological freedom is queerly reflected in Undine's discovery that each of her marriages is no more than another mode of imprisonment; and Undine's creator allows more than a hint that the young woman is as much a victim as an aggressor amid the assorted snobberies, tedium, and fossilized rules of conduct of American and, even more, French high society. Above all, Undine suggests what Edith Wharton might have been like if, by some dreadful miracle, all her best and most lovable and redeeming features had been suddenly cut away. . . .

II

In 1911, two years before *The Custom of the Country* was published, Wharton brought out the short novel that seems her most American story, the New England tragedy *Ethan Frome*. I would guess that it is now her most widely read book, and is likely to remain so. Certainly *Ethan Frome* is Wharton's only fiction to have become part of the American mythology, though it is hardly an early-twentieth-century *Scarlet Letter*. Relentless and stripped, *Ethan Frome* is tragedy not as Hawthorne wrote it, but in the mode of pain and of a reductive moral sadism, akin perhaps to Robert Penn Warren's harshness toward his protagonists, particularly in *World Enough and Time*. The book's aesthetic fascination, for me, centers in Wharton's audacity in touching the limits of a reader's capacity at absorbing really extreme suffering, when that suffering is bleak, intolerable, and in a clear sense unnecessary. Wharton's astonishing authority here is to render such pain with purity and economy, while making it seem inevitable, as much in the nature of things and of psyches as in the social customs of its place and time.

R. W. B. Lewis praises *Ethan Frome* as "a classic of the realistic genre"; doubtless it is, and yet literary "realism" is itself intensely metaphorical, as Lewis keenly knows. *Ethan Frome* is so charged in its representation of reality as to be frequently phantasmagoric in effect. Its terrible vividness estranges it subtly from mere naturalism, and makes its pain just bearable. Presumably Edith Wharton would not have said: "Ethan Frome—that is myself," and yet he is more his author than Undine Spragg was to be. Like Wharton, Ethan has an immense capacity for suffering, and an overwhelming sense of reality; indeed like Edith Wharton, he has too strong a sense of what was to be the Freudian reality principle.

Though an exact contemporary of Freud, Edith Wharton showed no interest in him, but she became an emphatic Nietzschean, and *Ethan Frome* manifests both a Nietzschean perspectivism, and an ascetic intensity that I suspect goes back to a

reading of Schopenhauer, Nietzsche's precursor. What fails in
Ethan, and in his beloved Mattie, is precisely what Schopenhauer
urged us to overcome: the Will to Live, though suicide was hardly
a Schopenhauerian solution. In her introduction to *Ethan Frome*,
Wharton states a narrative principle that sounds more like Balzac,
Browning, or James, but that actually reflects the Nietzsche of *The
Genealogy of Morals*:

> Each of my chroniclers contributes to the narrative *just so
> much as he or she is capable of understanding* of what, to
> them, is a complicated and mysterious case; and only the
> narrator of the tale has scope enough to see it all, to
> resolve it back into simplicity, and to put it in its rightful
> place among his larger categories.

But does Wharton's narrator have scope enough to see all of
the tale that is *Ethan Frome*? Why is the narrator's view more than
only another view, and a simplifying one at that? Wharton's introduction memorably calls her protagonists "these figures, my
granite outcroppings; but half-emerged from the soil, and scarcely
more articulate." Yet her narrator (whatever her intentions) lacks
the imagination to empathize with granite outcroppings who are
also men and women:

> Though Harmon Gow developed the tale as far as his
> mental and moral reach permitted there were perceptible
> gaps between his facts, and I had the sense that the deeper
> meaning of the story was in the gaps. But one phrase
> stuck in my memory and served as the nucleus about
> which I grouped my subsequent inferences: "Guess he's
> been in Starkfield too many winters."
>
> Before my own time there was up I had learned to
> know what that meant. Yet I had come in the degenerate
> day of trolley, bicycle and rural delivery, when communi-
> cation was easy between the scattered mountain villages,
> and the bigger towns in the valleys, such as Bettsbridge
> and Shadd's Falls, had libraries, theatres and Y. M. C. A.
> halls to which the youth of the hills could descend for

recreation. But when winter shut down on Starkfield, and the village lay under a sheet of snow perpetually renewed from the pale skies, I began to see what life there—or rather its negation—must have been in Ethan Frome's young manhood.

I had been sent up by my employers on a job connected with the big power-house at Corbury Junction, and a long-drawn carpenters' strike had so delayed the work that I found myself anchored at Starkfield—the nearest habitable spot—for the best part of the winter. I chafed at first, and then, under the hypnotising effect of routine, gradually began to find a grim satisfaction in the life. During the early part of my stay I had been struck by the contrast between the vitality of the climate and the deadness of the community. Day by day, after the December snows were over, a blazing blue sky poured down torrents of light and air on the white landscape, which gave them back in an intenser glitter. One would have supposed that such an atmosphere must quicken the emotions as well as the blood; but it seemed to produce no change except that of retarding still more the sluggish pulse of Starkfield. When I had been there a little longer, and had seen this phase of crystal clearness followed by long stretches of sunless cold; when the storms of February had pitched their white tents about the devoted village and the wild cavalry of March winds had charged down to their support; I began to understand why Starkfield emerged from its six months' siege like a starved garrison capitulating without quarter. Twenty years earlier the means of resistance must have been fewer, and the enemy in command of almost all the lines of access between the beleaguered villages; and, considering these things, I felt the sinister force of Harmon's phrase: "Most of the smart ones get away." But if that were the case, how could any combination of obstacles have hindered the flight of a man like Ethan Frome?

The narrator's "mental and moral reach" is not in question, but his vision has acute limitations. Winter indeed is the cultural issue, but *Ethan Frome* is not exactly Ursula K. LeGuin's *The Left Hand of Darkness*. It is not a "combination of obstacles" that hindered the flight of Ethan Frome, but a terrible fatalism which is a crucial part of Edith Wharton's Emersonian heritage. Certainly the narrator is right to express the contrast between the winter sublimity of: "a blazing blue sky poured down torrents of light and air on the white landscape, which gave them back in an intenser glitter," and the inability of the local population to give back more than sunken apathy. But Frome, as the narrator says on the novel's first page, is himself a ruined version of the American Sublime: "the most striking figure in Starkfield . . . his great height . . . the careless powerful look he had . . . something bleak and unapproachable in his face." Ethan Frome is an Ahab who lacks Moby-Dick, self-lamed rather than wounded by the white whale, and by the whiteness of the whale. Not the whiteness of Starkfield but an inner whiteness or blackness has crippled Ethan Frome, perhaps the whiteness that goes through American tradition "from Edwards to Emerson" and on through Wharton to Wallace Stevens contemplating the beach world lit by the glare of the Northern Lights in "The Auroras of Autumn":

> Here, being visible is being white,
> Is being of the solid of white, the accomplishment
> Of an extremist in an exercise . . .
>
> The season changes. A cold wind chills the beach.
> The long lines of it grow longer, emptier,
> A darkness gathers though it does not fall
>
> The whiteness grows less vivid on the wall.
> The man who is walking turns blankly on the sand.
> He observes how the north is always enlarging the change,
>
> With its frigid brilliances, its blue-red sweeps
> And gusts of great enkindlings, its polar green,
> The color of ice and fire and solitude.

That, though with a more sublime eloquence, is the visionary world of *Ethan Frome*, a world where the will is impotent, and tragedy is always circumstantial. The experiential puzzle of *Ethan Frome* is ultimately also its aesthestic strength: we do not question the joint decision of Ethan and Mattie to immolate themselves, even though it is pragmatically outrageous and psychologically quite impossible. But the novel's apparent realism is a mask for its actual fatalistic mode, and truly it is a northern romance, akin even to *Wuthering Heights*. A visionary ethos dominates Ethan and Mattie, and would have dominated Edith Wharton herself, had she not battled against it with her powerful gift for social reductiveness. We can wonder whether even *The Age of Innocence*, with its Jamesian renunciations in the mode of *The Portrait of a Lady*, compensates us for what Wharton might have written, had she gone on with her own version of the American romance tradition of Hawthorne and Melville.

Harold Bloom (b. 1930) is Sterling Professor of the Humanities at Yale University and one of America's leading literary critics. His works include *The Western Canon*, *A Map of Misreading*, and *Agon: Towards a Theory of Revisionism*. He also has edited more than 30 anthologies of literature and literary criticism.